Wilds of the Heart

Curiosity Bay Series #2

Karice Bolton

Edited by V. Clifton

Cover Design: Didi
Adobe Stock: © #Astronaut Images/KOTO

Interior: B&B Formatting
Adobe Stock: © Vodoleyka

DEDICATION

For those who have that small whisper in your heart. Let it scream into the wilds…

Chapter One

Emily

The adorable squirrel stared straight at me. His shoulders rose high as his dark eyes widened in fear. His little body shot straight up in the air, at least four feet up, as I worked the brakes on my scooter.

He hovered briefly in the air before landing squarely back on his feet, paralyzed by fear, when his instinct kicked in. The little guy skittered off the pavement to the sidewalk and up the maple tree as my pink scooter came to a screeching halt.

My heart raced with adrenaline, fear, and relief that I hadn't just squashed my favorite squirrel outside our family's antique store. Every morning, I always added food to the squirrel feeder as we shared a friendly, yet distant, greeting.

But this morning, it all could have been over.

One more little reminder about how fragile life could be. Ever since my grandma's death, I'd become acutely aware of loss. It had been several years, but I missed her fiercely.

I parked across from my family's antique store and took a deep breath, watching the little squirrel scamper along the limb above.

The town was waking up for the morning with shop doors opening, cafés bustling, and laughter echoing through the air as families wandered down the sidewalks to start their morning in town. Marigold Island was a magical place. The quirkiness of the island and the people had always been embraced, and our store was no different.

My sister, Amelia, whistled and shook her head as she stood on the sidewalk arranging a table of vintage pottery for sale. "Wow. That was a close call."

"Tell me about it," I called across the street as I pulled my matching pink helmet off and slid it into the seat compartment.

I glanced both ways and crossed the street to start

my day working at Baubles and Curiosities. I'd grown up helping out at the antique store, and it was a natural transition once I actually needed to make a living.

It kind of turned out that way for all my siblings, and I wouldn't say any of us minded it. Other than my brother Brad. I could never tell with him.

Right when I reached my sister, I noticed my newly-acquired BFF sitting on the green bench outside the antique store, taking everything in.

I narrowed my eyes at him. "Lucas Edwards, wipe that smirk off your face."

"I see your driving skills are as fantastic as ever." His eyes nearly sparkled as his gaze fastened on mine.

I felt a singe of electricity pulse through me as I lifted my eyes from his.

"Chester isn't a squirrel pancake, so that is a win for all parties involved." I grinned and spun around, feeling his gaze still on me.

"Chester?" Lucas's deep voice coated over me like a sticky candy I shouldn't want. "He has a name?"

I happily nodded. "They all do. There's Chester, Cinderella, Custard, Calico, and Cutie."

I glanced over my shoulder to see his smile only widen as he pulled his gaze away and shook his head.

A thrill shot through me, but I tamped it down as quickly as it came. Lucas was...

An amazing friend.

The best of friends, really.

I couldn't imagine anyone more loyal or devoted...

But he was an awful boyfriend.

Or I imagined him to be if history had a habit of repeating itself.

Which, if anything about the antiques business had rubbed off on me, it was to notice patterns... cycles.

And Lucas was full of patterns and cycles.

And most of them had to do with dating apps and weekend nights.

I reached for a Rookwood vase and picked it up, looking over at Amelia. "Should this really be outside on display?"

Amelia nodded. "It looks like a Rookwood piece, doesn't it?" She waggled her finger. "But it's not."

I stared at the floral motif wrapped around the

vase and nodded. "That's why you're paid the big bucks."

Our family's antique store had been a part of each and every one of us growing up. There wasn't a school day that went by when we weren't combing the shelves and looking at these found objects to pass the time after classes let out. But Amelia was the one who had a natural knack for finding the jewel in the middle of junk. She lived and breathed antiques.

I was just happy to have a job that let me stay on the island and read my books during slow times. Although, I did enjoy being surrounded by beautiful and quirky things. It was a perk of the job, but I tended to gravitate toward fanciful objects like an upside-down pink frog with three eyes that worked well as a soap dish.

But I had always been... quirky. I didn't need a lot to be happy.

One thing I loved to do on a Friday night was grab a good book, head to the bar, and immerse myself in the story between the pages while the world spun around me. I could eat some garlic fries, feel like I'd socialized, and head back home to finish my book. It was my dirty little secret, only because my family assumed I was out dancing the night away.

Amelia chuckled. "It's a fun piece from the 1950s, but it's not a Rookwood."

Lucas snickered, and I flashed him a wry smile.

"Why are you here, anyway? Don't you have to work or something?" My hand flew to my hip.

The truth was that he came from family money, and although he had several ventures that delivered him mailbox money, his schedule was pretty loose. I'd noticed he'd been stopping by more and more.

Lucas kicked out his feet and linked his fingers behind his head, stretching his long, lean, and very muscular body as his smile deepened. He looked extremely comfortable.

"My schedule opened up today, and I thought, who better to pester than my newly-acquired bestie?"

The shop pug snorted underneath Lucas's bench. Dottie stretched her paws before placing her chin on them for some shut-eye. She'd heard Lucas's stories many times.

"We've been friends for nearly a year." I turned

slowly with the vase still in my hand and eyed him. "Spill it. What did you do?"

Lucas frowned. "Can't a guy just stop by to visit his amazing friend?"

My brows lifted as Amelia chuckled and eyed me.

I stomped my foot. "Now, I know you're up to something."

The morning chill mingled with the warmth of the sun as I glanced toward the ferry terminal. The tourists would be arriving soon for the long weekend, and I wouldn't have time to entertain Lucas.

Not to mention, I had three chapters left of a mystery book I was dying to finish at lunch. I was literally counting down the seconds until I could steal away a few minutes to bury myself in the pages. It was also why Chester the squirrel could have been history. I couldn't stop daydreaming about the story I'd been reading. I was extremely close to finding out whether I was right or not about who stole a Monet and pulled the trigger while doing so.

And if I were completely honest, I was a little

distracted because I'd been stood up last night, and I couldn't shake the feeling that I was destined to be single for the rest of my life.

The whirring of a saw blade lifted me back to reality when I glanced down the sidewalk to see scaffolding and a man frantically cutting something underneath.

This just wasn't the Friday to play hooky with Lucas. The weekend would bring tons of tourists. My sister Mae's coffee shop was about to open next door. This was the start of our busy spring and summer season.

I loosened my backpack from my shoulder and let out a playful sigh. "Let me go put my things down inside, and you can tell me why you're actually here."

Lucas shot up from the bench and winked, which worried me. He followed me inside as I caught my mom pretending not to notice that Lucas was right behind me. She bent down at a jewelry counter and hummed to herself.

The antique store has been in the family for decades and brought me a sense of comfort. The trinkets on the glass shelves didn't have a sprig of dust on them, and the gleaming shelves themselves reflected the sense of pride our family took in this store. As with the rest of the store, the glass was spotless. A toy car from the 1940s had tipped over, and I instinctively put it upright.

"Good morning, Mrs. Evans." Lucas waved at my mom, who slowly emerged from the cabinet.

She gave a nod. "Good to see you, Lucas."

I flashed him a suspicious look as we wandered up the stairs to the offices. It felt like we were suddenly in high school and he was trying to butter up the parents.

Plopping my backpack on a chair, I spun around and stared at Lucas.

There was something so disarming about him. His dark hair and striking blue eyes were certainly easy to look at it, but it was the kindness behind his gaze that always pulled at me. He carried himself with so much ease and confidence that some could mistake it for cockiness, but I knew better.

Lucas wasn't cocky. He was merely confident. But women always gave him a hard time, thinking he was egotistical or a player. I knew this because I was one of those who thought the same until I peeled back some of his layers.

Not to say he didn't date his fair share of women.

His lip curled up slightly on the right side, just under his dimple.

"Okay, spill it. Why are you here at nine o'clock in the morning? You would have had to have gotten up at six just to make the ferry."

"Who said I needed to take the ferry?"

The sudden revelation unexpectedly tied knots in my belly. We were merely friends, so it didn't matter how he spent his nights.

But lately, I noticed…

"Why would you be on Marigold Island?" I crossed my arms over my chest when I remembered that he'd texted about his date last night.

Was that why he was so happy?

He got lucky?

Ooph.

Maybe this was why I never specialized in having the opposite sex as my BFF. I shouldn't care if he goes out with women. That was what he was supposed to do. That was what I was supposed to do.

But the idea of a good book always lured me more than the reality of the dating world. I loved nothing more than cracking open the book, smelling the fresh ink, and settling into whatever world I was exploring. Up until recently, I loved burying myself in romance, but about a year ago, I switched over to mysteries. About the time I met Lucas, actually. I just needed a change of scenery between the pages.

It didn't help that I had an uncanny ability to let the story tell me things that it didn't tell others. I might sound kooky, but it was true. Books spoke to me. The antiques spoke to Amelia, and books spoke to me. My grandma always said we were a family full of mystics, which sounded fanciful, even if it wasn't true. It was a nice thought, though.

So, when the books suddenly whispered to switch to mystery, I listened, and it had proven to save my sanity with Lucas around.

And especially because being stood up last night wasn't unusual. It usually happened on date two, as it happened last night. So, while Lucas was out gallivanting around, I twiddled my thumbs wondering what happened to Mr. Not-So-Wonderful.

Lucas cleared his throat, and I glanced over to see his dark brows arch. I noticed how the fine lines around his eyes crinkled. "Don't you remember I had a date last night?"

I rolled my eyes. "It's hard to keep track of your social calendar."

He smirked and took a step closer, and I had the sudden urge to stop breathing. I looked down at the old wooden floor and tried to focus. I had a list of things to do today at the store, and as much as I loved hanging out with Lucas, I couldn't start letting him distract me at my job.

Keeping my head bent, looking at the floor, I tried to sneak a glance at him, but he was staring right at me.

He touched my chin softly and laughed. "Well, the date last night was a disaster. It was messy, unpredictable. My date was a sloppy eater. We couldn't hold a conversation longer than a minute and a half. It felt like I was running after a toddler the entire time."

A giddiness swept through my veins, followed by

a deep sense of guilt.

I shouldn't wish bad dates on the man.

Grinning, my eyes met his. "I had a date of my own last night."

Lucas's eyes instantly grew huge. "Yeah?"

I scowled and swatted at him. "You don't have to sound so surprised."

He laughed and shook his head. "It's not that. You just always make a point of letting the world know that you're not interested."

My scowl deepened. "What do you mean?"

Lucas stepped a little closer, and if I moved even an inch, I could wind up in his arms. He cupped my chin with his thumb and index finger, and my chest tightened with something I had never felt before.

And at my age, that was puzzling. I should have felt it at least once by now.

I drew a slow breath and kept my eyes steady on his since his grasp ensured it.

He smiled. "You might as well wear a badge that reads, *Men Suck.*"

I gasped and shook my head, his hand falling

from my face.

"You don't suck," I blurted out.

He shook his head and ignored the compliment. "How'd the date go last night?"

My cheeks reddened. "He never showed up."

"What a jerk." Lucas shook his head. "You got stood up?"

I flinched and glanced through the open banister downstairs, hoping my mom didn't hear.

"Could you keep it down?"

"Sorry. I just can't imagine a guy doing that to you."

I snickered and shook my head, wrapping myself in my arms. "It's not the first time, and I'm sure it won't be the last. It always happens on date two. I must terrify them on date one, and they don't want to insult me to my face."

Lucas's expression fell, and he pulled me into him. "Are you serious? You couldn't terrify a mouse, Emily. You've never mentioned that to me before."

I cocked my head slightly and grinned, looking into his eyes.

I'd be lying to myself if I didn't admit that I liked being in his arms. "It's not exactly something I'm proud of. It's embarrassing."

"They're the embarrassment. Not you." He slowly let go, and I took a step back.

I grinned and grabbed his arm once more. "You're a good friend to have. Now, spill the beans. Why are you here?"

He nodded slowly, but his gaze lingered on mine for a second longer than I expected, sending a tingle through me.

Lucas was one of those guys who could just look at a person and make them feel like a million bucks.

Which was great unless you needed to keep things platonic.

He reached his hand into his back pocket and pulled out his wallet, letting out a deep breath.

"I happen to have two tickets to a book reading and signing in Seattle that you've been dying to attend. Someone by the name of Charles Teal?"

"What?" My foot stomped unexpectedly. "How? It's been sold out for months."

"I have my ways."

I reached for the tickets, and he pulled them away. "But there's a catch."

"What? Seriously? I'm actually reading this guy's latest release right now. I only have three chapters left." I shook my head. "Lay it on me. What's the catch?"

He dangled the tickets just out of reach, which wasn't too hard for him to do since he was well over six feet tall, and I was barely above five feet tall.

And then it hit me.

"Wait a second. Isn't that today?" I glanced at the clock and then at my desk piled high with items to price and place out on the floor. "I can't go."

He touched my cheek and smiled. "You *can* go because I cleared it with your mom and every single sibling you have. I knew you'd make excuses if I didn't."

I narrowed my eyes on him. "Fine. Tell me the catch. There's always one with you."

He smiled. "Yet time and again, you always agree."

I rolled my eyes and snorted on accident, which, had he not been my best friend, would have been mortifying.

"You have to go out to dinner with me after the event at my favorite place in Seattle."

"Why not back here? There's plenty of amazing restaurants on Marigold Island. How about Milo's Pub?"

"Maybe, but you just need to get out of your comfort zone a little," he offered. "City life isn't so bad."

I snickered and shook my head. "I did that plenty in college. I like it here, but fine. I'll have dinner with you in the big city."

He laughed and shook his head, handing me a ticket.

"The reading is at two o'clock, so if we leave here by noon, we should be fine." Lucas spun around and headed toward the stairs.

"How'd you get these tickets? Seriously. They were impossible to find." I touched my necklace and ran my fingers along my wildflower pendant. My mom had gifted us with something special upon our birth that was meant to guide us, and mine happened to be a wildflower. I always found myself reaching for it when Lucas was around.

He shrugged. "Just an old friend who owed me a favor. No biggie."

I smiled and shook my head as Lucas went down the stairs, leaving me to my pile of knickknacks.

That was the thing about Lucas. He was always full of surprises. But soon, I hoped, I'd have one of my own to share.

Chapter Two

Lucas

"Dear, God, man." I shook my head, holding my forehead in my palms. "I cannot keep doing this. It's literally eating me up from the inside out. I can feel every little cell of my body getting chewed up and spat out before moving on to the next piece of me to do the same. Every second is torture." I looked up at my cousin and stared at him. "There will be nothing left of me by the end of this."

James rolled his eyes and laughed. "Don't be so dramatic."

I sat up and glared at my cousin. "You don't understand what it's like to be put in the friend zone by a woman who makes your knees weak and your world stand still."

"Listen, if it's meant to be, it will be." He shrugged.

"That's it?" I laughed, staring at him in disbelief. "That's your advice?"

James brushed his short beard with his thumb and looked toward the water. I'd driven to his place to pass the time and get some brotherly advice from the next best thing, my cousin. He moved in with Amelia, and it was the perfect place for them. His son had his own spacious bedroom, and then there were two other guest rooms, one that I frequented a lot when I babysat my nephew, like last night. Technically, he wasn't my nephew, but my cousin was my best friend, and being an uncle fit my duties.

But Amelia and James had it easy. They knew they liked each other.

With Emily, it wasn't like that. She saw me squarely as a friend.

I was fighting a losing battle.

But the more time I spent around her, the more I wanted her.

"So, why are you here if the girl you like is over

there?" He pointed toward the front door.

"I can't just follow her around for three hours like a lost puppy dog. I have to exude confidence and give her the feeling I have other places to be, other people to see."

James's right brow quirked. "Dude, it doesn't need to be that hard."

I waggled my finger at my cousin. "That's where you're wrong."

He grimaced and took a sip of coffee. "I just don't think it needs to be this complicated. Tell her how you feel."

My head tilted. "Right. Like I haven't thought of that."

"Okay, then what did she say?"

I straightened in my chair. "She laughed and told me she was just the next new, shiny object. That I'd get over it."

"Ouch." He chuckled. "She could have a point. How do you know you're not just into her because she's the first woman to put you in your place?"

I frowned. "What's that supposed to mean?"

"Think about it. The very first time we met Amelia and Emily, Emily told you off."

Chuckling, I shook my head. "Technically, I think she told you off first."

"And has a woman ever done that to you?"

"Only after a breakup," I confirmed. "But that's not why I'm drawn to Emily. She's vivacious, funny, gorgeous, smart, and…"

Perfect. Emily was absolutely perfect in every way.

Her dark hair and brilliant green eyes complemented one another in an ethereal way. Every time I glanced at her, I couldn't help but notice the glimmer in her gaze as playfulness lurked behind her expression.

She had three sisters, Audrey, Amelia, and May, plus a brother named Brad, who all looked incredibly related, but Emily stood out from them all by far.

"What if she'd fallen all over you? Would you still be crazy about her?" my cousin asked.

"Yeah. It's Emily. I just… like her." I smiled. "But because she's Emily, she never would fall over herself over a guy."

"Maybe so."

"Do you know what she told me this morning?"

"What?"

"She got stood up. Who in their right mind would do that to Emily?" The thought made my blood boil.

"Maybe it wasn't the person's fault?"

"I didn't get that impression from her."

I glanced outside to see the gentle ocean breeze shoving the clouds from the blue sky. It would be a good day to go over to Seattle, an easy ferry ride.

"So, are you going to tell her how you got those tickets for today?"

I froze, shrugging off the unsettling feeling. "Did you tell her sister?"

"It hasn't come up, but if it does, I'm not going to keep it from her."

I nodded. "Yeah. I get it. I'll bring it up."

"It shouldn't matter, right? You both are *just* friends." James smiled.

"Good point."

"Maybe it's a good test," my cousin offered.

"I don't think testing a relationship is exactly a brilliant idea."

James chuckled, standing up to stretch. "You're probably right about that."

"Has Amelia ever said anything?"

James walked toward the kitchen. "About what?" He kept his gaze forward and scratched the back of his head.

I could tell he was avoiding eye contact, which I took as a good sign.

Maybe Emily had talked to her sister about me.

But then, why wouldn't my cousin tell me?

Unless what Emily said wasn't good.

I grabbed my empty coffee mug and made my way to the kitchen as James poured himself another cup.

Waiting until James looked at me, I shoved my mug toward him to pour me some more coffee. "About me?"

James groaned. "I hate being in the middle."

"You're not in the middle. It's not like I'm asking you to set us up. We're already friends. We text daily. We hang out. I'm just hoping to find out if she's ever dropped a hint to her sister about me."

James poured coffee into my mug and sighed. "She's mentioned you a time or two. Mostly, when you two first met. She hasn't said anything recently."

"And?" I raised my full mug.

"She said you were infuriatingly handsome but not boyfriend material."

My shoulders slumped in defeat, and I put my mug down.

James grimaced, patting my shoulder. "I'm sure she's changed her mind."

I chuckled and shook my head, picking up my mug. "No. That's still very much the vibe I'm getting."

"Don't ask me things if you don't want the answer." He clanked his mug with mine.

"I'll remember that. Besides, I think I can change her mind."

"That's the spirit. Just wear her down until she's exhausted."

"Exactly." I pointed at him with my index finger and took a sip of my coffee.

"I do think you might want to tell her how you

got those tickets, though. Just sayin'."

I sucked in a breath and let it out slowly, knowing he was right. "I will. When the time is right." I glanced at my phone. "I should get going, though."

"Oh, and thanks for babysitting Henry last night."

"Of course." I smiled, thinking back to Henry. He was a fun kid. "You know I'll drop everything for him."

"Does Emily you were watching him last night?"

"No. She thinks I had a date."

James chuckled. "Does she think that every time you watch him?"

I shot him a wry grin. "Possibly."

"No wonder she thinks you're a player."

"Come to find out, I'm just a really good babysitter."

My cousin laughed and gave me a quick knuckle punch, and I made my way out of the kitchen and down the hall to the front door. I always liked being able to joke around with my cousin. We'd been best friends since we were kids. But since he'd started dating Amelia and I'd started crushing on her sister, I'd noticed things had changed a little bit.

I didn't know if it was on me or if James was hiding something from me about Emily. Or if I were just a hopeless romantic stuck in a player's body. I shut the door behind me and got into my car. The antique store was only a few minutes away, but I didn't have to be there for an hour.

Instead of taking a right toward town, I took a left and drove toward the beach where my family would spend time whenever we visited my grandparents' orchard. There was the tiniest sliver of sand at this reserve, but the shoreline was mostly pebbled and rocky. I found a place to park in a small lot above the ocean and made my way down to the beach.

I'd taken Emily here a few times. Each time grew more special than the last, and I could never put my finger on why.

But that was how it was with Emily. Each encounter grew into something more to be treasured, which was why I didn't want to lose having her in my life.

The waves lapped gently against the stones as I

stared out toward the inky-blue water. I found a boulder to sit on and let out a deep breath as thoughts of Emily wound their way back into my mind.

Sometimes, it felt like Emily and I were an old married couple. She'd throw jabs at me that I pretended didn't sting, and I'd tease her about something trivial in return. Other times, it felt like she saw right through me and understood my vulnerabilities but never threatened to exploit them, just like a true friend.

Maybe that was why we'd become such fast friends.

Perhaps that was all we were meant to be.

But lately, she'd started writing poetry, and I swear that every time she shared a poem with me, it sounded like us.

Some version of us.

Or maybe that was just wishful thinking.

I moved my fingers through my hair, wishing away the monotony of being single, and leaned back against the rock. The coldness of the boulder soaked through my shirt as I thought about what I really wanted.

Was James right?

Was I only interested in Emily because she'd turned me down a million times?

But I'd never seriously asked her out, either. It was only in passing or in jest because I knew where she'd planted me.

In the vast platonic wasteland.

I remember my grandpa always used to tease me that I'd be a fifty-year-old bachelor, and when I was sixteen, that didn't sound all that bad, but now that I was thirty-five, it sent a cold chill through me. The thought of being alone in fifteen years was depressing. It didn't help that James found his forever and had somehow put me in the category of the perennial bachelor.

I was like the fun uncle, the great babysitter, and the sidekick.

Emily saw me as all that, too. We'd even babysat Henry together, but none of that seemed to show her that I could actually be…

Well, I didn't know what she wanted me to be other than a friend.

My hope had been with getting these tickets today that she'd see me as a guy who cared for her, listened to her, and would go above and beyond for her.

The unfortunate part of the whole thing was definitely how I obtained the tickets, and if Emily and I were dating, it could be seen as a prickly topic.

But we weren't together.

So, it shouldn't matter.

I stared at the waves coming to the shore and propped myself off the rock.

Things didn't always have to be complicated and messy, and my friendship with Emily was definitely neither of those things. It was solid, stable, and nearly perfect.

Except that there wasn't a moment that went by where I didn't want to pull her into my arms and feel her lips against mine.

I smiled to myself and moved off the rock, making my way to my car. Things didn't have to be difficult between Emily and me, and I wasn't going to start now. She was a phenomenal best friend, and that was plenty for now.

It would have to be.

As I made my way back to my car, my phone

buzzed, and I saw a text come over that made my stomach tense.

Looks like I'll be able to get to the signing after all. See ya there.

"Things don't have to be messy," I repeated under my breath. "But I sure as heck had better tell Emily how I got the tickets."

I shoved the phone into my pocket and climbed into my car, trying to push away the worrisome feeling.

By the time I got to the antique store, I knew my old life had caught up with me. But that didn't mean I needed to tell Emily everything.

We were only friends.

As I yanked on the door to the store, the little bell jangled, and all eyes turned in my direction. Every Evans sister happened to be at the store. I didn't spot their brother, Brad, thankfully.

There were times when I wasn't sure he liked me.

"The hero of the moment," Emily's mom shouted from behind the counter.

Amelia chuckled as her gaze caught mine while Emily wandered toward the front of the store with a porcelain poodle in her arms.

"There you are," Emily sang out. "I thought maybe you got cold feet."

I scowled. "Cold feet?"

Emily's long, dark lashes outlined her vibrant green eyes, and the hint of red gloss on her lips distracted me just enough to forget her family was around.

Almost.

"James said you'd left our house an hour ago," Amelia explained.

"Ah, right. The tattle tale." I grinned. "There's no hiding anything on this island."

Emily laughed, which made my insides toss and turn like a sinking ship. I was doomed. Everything about her was insanely attractive.

But I could do this. I could be the dutiful friend. We'd been doing it for nearly a year, this back and forth.

"Speaking of, you still haven't told me how you got the tickets." Emily set the porcelain poodle on a table and smiled at me.

Emily was so damn pretty. She took a step forward, sending another look in my direction. Something about her eyes always made me feel like I was where I belonged, right in front of her.

I tore my gaze away and shook my head. "I can't tell you all my secrets, or you won't find me mysterious and alluring."

She laughed. "You're about as mysterious as a pot scrubber."

"What does that even mean?"

She wandered over toward me. "I don't know, but it's what popped out. Are you ready?"

I glanced at her mom, who was eyeing us, and nodded. "Absolutely. And dinner in Seattle, right?"

She groaned. "Are you sure we can't do Milo's down the street?"

Amelia chuckled. "It's true. Emily does spend most Friday nights whooping it up there. I think she has a crush on Rick, the bartender."

Emily threw a withering look in her sister's direction, which only made her sister grin wider.

"And the last time we were there together, he

asked you out," she added.

Her sister Audrey came down from the upstairs offices and waved.

"When was that?" I asked, trying to act like it didn't matter. Only the question itself said otherwise.

Emily spun around and stared at me. "Long before I met you, but it's still my favorite place on a Friday night when I'm not busy babysitting Henry. And their garlic fries are amazing."

"A promise is a promise. Dinner in Seattle or we aren't meeting your author crush."

Her cheeks reddened, and she grabbed her purse from her sister. "He's not my crush. I don't have crushes."

"Not even on the bartender?" I chuckled, squeezing Emily's shoulder as we wandered out the door with her ignoring me. "Of course, you don't. You just have friends."

Chapter Three

Emily

The line went down the sidewalk as we impatiently waited to get inside. I adjusted my backpack and smiled at Lucas, who suddenly looked a little uncomfortable, which was completely unlike him.

I slipped my thumb under the strap and shifted my weight, staring at Lucas.

"What's up? You look like you've seen a ghost."

Lucas scratched his chin and smiled before shaking his head. "I do?"

"Yup." I popped the 'p' and followed his gaze down the street to see a beautiful brunette in a short, pink miniskirt and a white midriff camisole.

"Ah, gotcha. I'm surprised she reads." I glanced at Lucas, who smiled and brought his gaze to mine. I couldn't believe those words rolled off my tongue. I touched my wildflower necklace and drew a breath.

Lucas grinned, tilting his chin as his eyes locked on mine. "Since when did you start judging a book by its cover?"

I chuckled, noticing the line had started to move. "Always. That's how I knew you weren't the settling down type." I winked at him as we slowly made our way toward the entrance.

I glanced down at my worn jeans, pink gingham top, and white Converse sneakers. It was awesome that I wasn't trying to compete with the woman staring at Lucas because there was no competition.

She flat-out won. She was gorgeous and put together and... gorgeous. Did I mention that?

Another wonderful benefit of being friends and only friends. What I wore didn't matter. There was no competition.

No competition at all.

In fact, one of my favorite lines from my current book was something like, *"In the quiet hours of night, there is no light to see the rivals that should never be."*

The words made me smile. I loved the visual.

It was why I'd started playing with poetry myself.

Writing poems didn't come easily for me, but it was something I enjoyed apart from reading, which was why I'd done what I'd done and hadn't told a soul.

Not even Lucas. It would just have to wait until I got my reply, even though I was dying to tell him.

"You've got me pegged all wrong, Emily," he teased. "I just haven't convinced the woman I'm hopelessly in love with that I'm a changed man."

His eyes remained fastened on mine, and electricity zapped through me, landing in my belly to smolder and promptly fizzle out.

I pulled my gaze from his and shrugged. "Well, I'm sure the lucky lady will pull through for you. In fact, here she comes."

"Lucas Edwards, I'd recognize you anywhere."

I looked up from the pavement and saw the miniskirt woman waving frantically in our direction as she nearly floated over.

I never understood how women could walk like

that. My gate was more of a thump, clog, swoosh step, but more power to the refined ladies of the world.

Lucas tensed, but a smile lined his expression. It wasn't the kind of smile I was used to from him. This one was forced and drawn out extra wide.

"Tickets," a friendly sales clerk called out. She was standing by the door, gesturing for us to move forward.

Lucas handed the tickets to her as we all made our way inside, miniskirt included.

"When you didn't respond to my text earlier, I thought I might not see you after all." She grinned, barely giving a glance in my direction.

I readjusted my backpack straps and slung it in front of me, fishing my book out of my bag.

"Lydia, this is Emily." Lucas's voice cut through my pseudo-concentration as I grabbed the book and looked up at the woman.

She pursed her lips together and nodded without a word.

"Nice to meet you," I said, smiling.

"Likewise." Her voice was flat, like her gaze,

until she looked back at Lucas. "I'm so happy we get to connect again. What are the odds that I'm here with my client and you actually reached out?"

I cocked my head slightly and smiled at Lucas, who looked extremely uncomfortable.

"So, I never pegged you for a mystery reader. You always struck me as the guy who goes out and parties in the city with the coffee table books never cracked open in your living room."

I chuckled and slapped his back. "You're right. He's the partier, and I'm the reader."

But I thought her judgment was a little harsh as she eyed me.

Lydia's expression changed. "Oh, you're together, you two."

"No." I shook my head as Lucas stared straight ahead. "We're just friends."

She let out an exasperated sigh. "Phew. I reached out to Clara last night to tell her I heard from you."

Clara?

My gaze flew to his, and I watched his jaw tense as he drew in a steady breath.

"Did you know she's single now? She and Jimmy broke up about a year ago. Clara's back in the state again..." She let her voice trail off and eyed me before bringing her gaze back to Lucas. "Her son wanted to come out here to college, so she decided to move back so she's closer to friends and family. He's finishing high school here."

Lucas nodded and glanced at me before turning his attention back to Lydia. "Thanks for pulling through for me on these tickets."

"Of course. It's a great excuse to catch up with you after all these years."

Lucas glanced at me with an apologetic look in his gaze, which was quite amusing because I didn't have a clue what was actually going on or who this woman was.

"Emily is a huge fan of this author," Lucas explained.

Lydia checked her phone and looked up at me.

I nodded in agreement, clutching my book. "It's a dream, actually. Somebody pinch me."

Anybody, really.

Because I do not know what is going on here.

The seats were filling up, and my stomach started roiling with worry as I watched the crowd converging on the area.

"I'm going to go find a seat," I told Lucas, touching his arm softly.

Lydia's gaze drilled into me as Lucas nodded, replying, "I'll come with you."

"No need to rush." Lydia shook her head. "Those two tickets are reserved for the front row."

My heart jumped as I looked at Lucas in surprise. "Wow. Thank you. I didn't even know you could get tickets like that."

Whoever you may be.

"My pleasure. It's a perk of the business. I usually don't come to my clients' readings when they're seasoned vets like Charles, but I wanted to catch up with Clara and the gang. I'm having drinks with them later."

She reached out and squeezed Lucas's arm. "You should come."

"I have plans, but thanks." Lucas's lips pressed into a thin line.

"No, you should go." I nodded, glancing at Lydia. "Really. How often is the gang all together?" I tried to hold in a chuckle as I thought about the one and only thing that I knew from Lucas's high school years.

He hated that period of his life.

And I'd certainly never heard of any gang he loved to be a part of from then.

"Clara would just die if you showed up." Lydia's head bounced up and down.

Lucas shook his head and touched my shoulder, slowly moving his hand down my spine. An unexpected delight shot through me as I felt a little push toward the seating area.

"Not tonight, Lydia. But I appreciate the invite."

She let out a dramatic sigh and rolled her eyes. "I hope you don't mind, but I gave Clara your number."

Lucas stopped moving, and his eyes snapped to Lydia's. "Lydia, I appreciate the tickets. I do, but I've moved on from high school."

"I—" Lydia snapped her mouth closed and nodded. "Sorry, I just... they say time heals all. I just assumed you'd gotten over it."

I eyed Lucas as I felt the gentle pressure of his fingertips on my back.

The carefree, fun-loving friend had been replaced with a guy who desperately wanted to get out of this situation, and that was what friends were for.

"Thanks again for the tickets," I told Lydia, looping my fingers with Lucas's as we started toward the seats. We fell in step together as we moved deeper into the bookstore.

"As usual, books save the day," I whispered.

When we were far enough away, I spun around to look at him. "But what in the world was that? And why don't you just go hang out with them?"

Lucas smiled as we took a seat in the front row.

"It's a bit more complicated than that."

I slid my backpack under the seat and held my book on my lap as I inhaled the amazing scent of freshly printed books. Large posters dangled in front of us as I eagerly waited for the author's appearance.

But I couldn't help but wonder what made Lucas so squirmy a few minutes ago. I snuck a look at him, and he was staring straight ahead at the empty chair reserved for the author.

"You okay? We can take off if you want."

Lucas looked at me and smiled. "No way. This is too important."

"You sure?" I pointed over my shoulder. "Because whatever just happened back there kind of stole your mojo."

His brows quirked up, and I saw the familiar, relaxed smile return to his expression. "Mojo?"

"What? Like it's a surprise? Mojo usually just oozes from you."

Lucas let out a deep breath and shook his head. "You always know how to make me feel better."

I studied Lucas for a brief second, wondering who Clara was and what had happened back in high school that made him so uncomfortable.

Granted, that period in my life was like a rollercoaster too.

Heartbreak.

Mortification.

Isolation.

The usual.

Thundering applause drifted over the room as I turned my attention to the front to see Charles wandering to his chair. He wore a green fedora, chinos, and a blue button-down shirt. He scanned the audience and looked happy to be here, which made it even more thrilling.

As he took a seat, he brought his eyes toward the audience and began speaking about his latest release.

I should be clinging to his every word, but I couldn't. I snuck a peek at Lucas, and there was no denying that whatever baggage Lydia had handed him with these tickets wasn't worth it.

My hand slid to his knee in a comforting gesture as I tried to keep focused on Charles. The crowd laughed, and I realized I couldn't pay attention because I just wanted to make sure that Lucas was okay.

Lucas linked his hand with mine and smiled as I rested my head on his shoulder. If anyone glanced over, they might think we were a couple.

The ease of his hand in mine and the closeness we shared had always come easily. I could effortlessly tease him while simultaneously pushing down my feelings for him.

Just like tonight.

But it was because we'd been instant friends and nothing more. The moment his cousin dated my sister, we just bonded. Sometimes over silliness and one-line insults, but it was a bond, nonetheless.

So, Clara wasn't my business. However, I couldn't pretend that I wasn't interested. Whoever she was, she struck a nerve with Lucas, and I hadn't ever seen that before with him.

Very little ever ruffled his feathers. I think that's why we hit it off so well and was precisely why our friendship grew so strong so quickly. He didn't get offended by my observations.

A lot of people did.

Perhaps, that was why I preferred fictional men to real ones.

But it didn't help that Lucas was easy on the eyes and could even make a nun's imagination run wild.

Honestly, it was for the best that he was a player. It protected my heart before it ever had a chance to get scuffed up a bit.

Friendship was easy.

But right now, I wanted to know more than anything what made Lucas so uptight.

I forced myself to listen to my favorite author of all time since it was my fault that we were here in the first place.

I slid another look at Lucas and could tell his mind was a million miles away.

The crowd laughed, and I watched the author stand up, adjust his hat, and smile before pointing at a stack of his books.

"I know how hard it was to get tickets to tonight's event. Thank you for that, but it also tells me you've probably already read my latest release. So, spoiler alert. The nurse pulled the trigger."

I gasped in horror, and the entire room went silent, turning their attention to me.

I had three chapters left.

Three!

"Miss, are you okay?" Charles asked.

"Sorry. I… I had three chapters left to read, and I was certain it was the brother."

Everyone chuckled as Charles nodded in

sympathy. "I'm only teasing. I would never give anything away like that."

I covered my heavily beating chest and let out a sigh of relief as Lucas pulled me into him, dropping his lips to my ear.

"You're so cute. If only I could make you gasp like that."

Heat instantly flooded through me as my cheeks reddened. Every cell in my body ignited with the emotion I'd been hiding from him and myself.

I looked up at him as his eyes locked on mine and teased, "Maybe you'll get lucky tonight."

He looked at me, puzzled. "Wait. What?"

Mortification pulsed through me at a fiery speed.

Oh, no.

That wasn't what he'd said.

"I need to pluck something tonight." I ran my finger over my left brow, wishing I were a better poet.

"Uh, okay..." He glanced at my brows and whispered, "This is getting weird."

My eyes widened, and I shook my head. "No, I mean... what did you say?"

Lucas leaned closer and whispered, "I said, if only I could wear a hat like that."

Okay. So definitely not, 'If only I could make you gasp like that'.

I clenched my eyes closed, bringing my attention back to the author. "Right. Totally. That's what I meant. Maybe you'll find one just like that later," I whispered. "Who knows? You could get lucky."

A smile touched Lucas's lips, and he nodded, pulling me in. "Maybe."

And that was why I never got to date number two, but thankfully, I wasn't dating Lucas. Just creeping him out.

Charles picked up his latest novel and cracked it open as he began reading my favorite first sentence ever, but all I could think about was how much I wished Lucas had said that.

Chapter Four

Lucas

I looked around the bookstore and didn't see Lydia as Emily looped her arm around mine and glanced up at me while adjusting her backpack.

She winked at me, showing me the author's autograph before sliding it into her bag. "You are the best friend a girl could ask for. You know that, right?"

Chuckling, I shrugged. "Tell me again."

"You're the best friend a girl could ask for."

I laughed, squeezing her closer before we made it outside. The crisp air hit my face as we stepped onto the sidewalk, so I pulled her tighter.

Spring in Seattle had a funny way of vacillating between winter and summer, and the temperatures were dipping quickly.

Her pink gingham shirt wasn't enough to keep her warm tonight and the café was a few doors down. My eyes hovered on her shirt a little too long when I noticed a couple of buttons undone. I tore my gaze away and focused on tonight.

I could still pull this off.

Tell her how I felt.

But just having her in my arms felt good, and the feeling completely turned around the night. I still couldn't believe Lydia had given my number to Clara. That part of my life was over.

So over.

I kissed the top of Emily's head before I even realized what I was doing. She threw her gaze to mine and chuckled.

"What put you in a good mood so suddenly?" I noticed her touching her wildflower necklace. I'd finally figured out that she had a habit of doing that when she was nervous or uncertain.

I looked down the sidewalk and smiled. "You."

"Me?"

I pulled her in, and she laughed as I felt her small

frame against me.

We probably looked like two friends just having a fun night, laughing and walking down a bustling sidewalk.

But I wanted so much more.

And tonight, I'd planned on telling her that.

Until Lydia.

I wanted tonight to be perfect, but I knew things got complicated the moment Lydia mentioned Clara.

It wasn't that Emily even blinked an eye over it, but I knew she'd bring it up.

And I didn't readily have an explanation.

Not tonight.

The well-lit streets reflected the lively crowds going into the restaurants, cafes, and bars that lined the street.

But I couldn't help but worry I'd run into the people Lydia had mentioned.

And that was just it. They were just people. I didn't know them any longer. I apparently didn't know them well then, either.

Especially Clara.

My chest tightened at the thought of everything I'd gone through at seventeen.

Not even James knew.

I could still pull this off and confess my feelings to Emily.

Emily's gaze caught mine. "So, where are you taking me? I'm freezing and starving."

"Two doors down. Red awning," I told her, wrapping my arm over her shoulders to shutter the wind from her.

She curled into me as we walked in unison down the sidewalk, playfully dodging other couples and dogs until we hit the café.

"Oh, nice. I guess getting off the island now and again is okay to do."

I chuckled, letting go of her long enough to open the door for her. She ducked inside and did a little shiver as the hostess looked over at us with a smile.

"You're just saying that because you can smell the garlic," I teased.

Her eyes widened into the pouty, playful expression that always drove me crazy. "What do they say about that? It drives away the vampires and dates?"

"Something like that."

I told the hostess how many, and she led us toward a table in the corner overlooking the bustling sidewalk.

The signing that took place right after the reading was quick, and we'd already managed to beat the after-work and dinner crowd.

"It smells so good in here," Emily said, beaming. "Is it bad that I'm on a natural high from earlier?"

Her eyes looked dizzy with excitement, and there was a small part of me that wished I could drive that same look out of her.

I smiled, opening the menu.

Maybe she had forgotten about the earlier run-in.

She looked up at me and grinned. "Okay, I just have to tell you."

"What?" I asked, watching her eyes dance with joy. "You're madly in love with me? Can't wait to run away with me?"

Emily chuckled and shook her head. "No way, silly. You're far too experienced for my fragile soul. This is more… personal."

I put down the menu and kept my gaze on hers. This was why I loved spending time with Emily. She was always full of surprises.

"I've been writing poetry."

My brows knitted together as I nodded. "I know. You've shared some poems with me, and they're beautiful."

Her cheeks flushed. "Thank you." She let out a long sigh. "I wasn't going to tell anyone until I heard back, in case it didn't happen."

"In case what didn't happen?"

Her eyes stayed on mine. "You have to promise not to tell anyone because if it doesn't work out, then nobody will know that I wasn't good enough."

"Emily, what are you talking about? You're amazing."

She grinned. "Well, I might be amazing, but that doesn't mean my poetry is."

"Trust me. It is."

"Okay. I submitted to a residency program for poetry. It's three months of pure solitude, poetry workshops, and writing time. I'd be leaving behind Marigold Island for three entire months, all expenses paid."

My jaw dropped. "Whoa, Emily. I had no idea that's what you wanted to do."

A wry grin sprang onto her lips. "I didn't either, but I saw the posting and thought, why not give it a go? I have nothing holding me here, and I can come back when it's all done."

A knot formed in my stomach, but I nodded, smiling. "Yeah. Totally. I'm excited for you."

She cocked her head slightly. "Please, just don't tell anyone. I'd be embarrassed if I didn't get it."

"You have my word, but even if you don't get selected, that doesn't mean your poetry isn't worthy."

She nodded, and her gaze fell to the table, but all I could think about was how the timing of everything was suddenly unraveling.

"So, that's my secret."

"That's a biggie." I looked out the window onto the sidewalks filling up with workers walking to their apartments and headed out for happy hours. "What will you do if you don't see my face all the time?"

She pretended to whistle. "I'll live. It'll be tough, though." Emily winked at me, and my insides tightened up.

Now really wasn't the time to drop this bomb on her. I didn't want anything to hold her back because I knew just how good her poems were.

"It's a complete longshot," she added, "but I'm following my heart."

"You have to do that." I smiled, taking her in. "I'm proud of you."

"Thank you."

Laughter rang out from the bar area near the back, and Emily opened her menu, glancing toward the noisy group.

"Isn't that Lydia?" Emily asked, peering over the menu at me.

My blood froze, and then I heard it.

Clara's laughter.

It hadn't changed since high school.

Emily's brows furrowed. "You okay?"

"Yeah, why would you ask?"

"Because you look like you're going to be sick. Do you want to leave?"

I shook my head and drew in a slow breath. This was ridiculous. It all happened so long ago.

My eyes stayed on Emily's. "No, I want to spend an incredible evening with you. It's not easy to find good friends and…"

She nodded. Her eyes smiled before her lips did, and she reached over, touching my hand with hers.

"Let me know if you change your mind and want to get out of here. I mean it." Emily squeezed my hand and glanced at the group. "Now, let's order some calamari. I'm about to faint."

The vividness in her gaze made me forget about everything from my past and focus on only her.

But that was the power Emily held over me. Whenever I was with her, nothing else mattered. It was why I'd be the best friend she'd ever had forever if it meant not jeopardizing my ability to see her.

It probably sounded crazy.

"Let's do some bruschetta, too," she said, closing the menu. "I've decided on the prawns and linguini. You might have to roll me out of here."

"I have no problem doing that." I decided on the filet and put the menu down as the server came over.

I ordered a bottle of wine and placed our appetizer order as I noticed Emily sneaking a peek at the boisterous group at the bar. It was only a matter of time before she brought them up.

"Was meeting Charles everything you'd dreamed of and more?" I teased.

She leaned onto the table and twisted her mouth into a contemplative pout. "Honestly? I'm kind of underwhelmed."

The surprise of her answer made me laugh. "How so?"

"I don't know." She shrugged. "Maybe it was the hat. Or… I don't know. I just expected my mystery writer to be hunched over in a corner, wearing a worn old cardigan, typing away, and coming up with eerie scenes in a darkened room, only the flicker of a fireplace lighting his keyboard and an untouched cup of tea next to him. Then…he emerges…I thought he might be a little hunched over, shielding his eyes from the light." She grinned. "Seeing him so… animated completely blew my thoughts out of the water."

"So, you were expecting the Hunchback of Notre Dame?" My mouth dropped open, and I shook my head. "Wow. Those are some interesting expectations."

She shrugged. "What can I say? I'm bonkers. I can't turn my mind off. Did you know that I do that with everyone I meet, read about, or see on television? Doesn't matter. Nobody is safe. It's like I'm psychic, but I have no actual talent because nine times out of ten, I'm wrong. I cannot read people for diddly squat." Emily licked her lips and cleared her throat. "I mean, look at you. I thought you were a total jerk, and you're the biggest sweetheart of them all."

I snickered and shook my head as the server brought our drinks and appetizers. "Well, good to know."

She flashed a wicked grin in my direction. "What? It's not like I hid that. You know what I thought about you."

I nodded, taking a sip of wine. "Yeah. You made those thoughts loud and clear."

Emily glanced toward the bar. "So, tell me what's up with Lydia and her buddy Clara? Or is she your buddy?"

My entire body tensed.

"It's all water under the bridge." I shrugged. "Just a bunch of bad high school memories."

Laughter rose from the bar, but I kept my gaze on Emily.

"You strike me as a guy who would have had a great high school experience. I was surprised when you told me it wasn't that great a few months back."

I was surprised she remembered. The comment was an off-handed sentence.

"What makes you think that?"

"Well, you're easy on the eyes, and I'm sure all the girls swooned in your direction." She laughed. "You were athletic, your family was wealthy, and you've got a great personality." Her brows waggled up and down. "Sounds pretty fantastic compared to a lot of kids."

I laughed. "Speaking of, how was your high school experience?"

She took a sip of wine and stretched her delicate

arms toward the ceiling. Her blouse pulled up, revealing her stomach.

I brought my gaze up to hers, and she cocked her head slightly, watching me. "My high school experience was not as great as my siblings'. Let's put it that way."

"How so?"

She shrugged. "There were good moments and bad moments. The high school on the island is pretty small, so we all knew each other. One foolish teenage misstep and everyone knew about it. I think that's why I love reading so much. I just stayed home and read instead of going to parties. But I think a lot of people thought I was stuck up when I was actually just shy and awkward."

I shook my head in disbelief. "I can't imagine you ever being shy."

She chuckled. "No, you're right. I wasn't really shy in that sense. I just learned to keep my mouth shut because whenever I said something, it was misconstrued." She took a sip of wine. "Or maybe I was just too direct."

"You? Too direct?" I laughed, shaking my head.

"Never."

"So, anyway… Apart from the normal teenage angst, high school was fine. It wasn't great, but it was fine. Lonely? Yeah. But I had my siblings. You?"

"I had my cousin and lots of friends, who turned out to be…" I shrugged. "Not so great."

"Really." She leaned in, glancing toward the bar. "Spill the tea."

I chuckled and shook my head. "Nah. It's all so long ago that it doesn't really matter. I just learned a lot about people."

"Women?" she asked.

And just like that, Emily could peel back the layers of my soul. She saw through me in an instant.

"My experience might have colored things a little for me." I nodded, taking a bite of bruschetta while she piled her plate with calamari.

"I hate these ones with the little tentacles." She stabbed one and wiggled it around a little, and I laughed before she put it on my plate. "So, tell me what happened with this *Clara* girl." She whispered the name *Clara* and kept her eyes on me.

"Typical teenage stuff." I kept my eyes locked on Emily's. I knew I couldn't look away, or she'd call my bluff.

But the truth of it was that I didn't feel like dredging up old feelings, stories, and everything in between while Clara stood fifty feet away. Not because I still had feelings for her. Those went away the moment she betrayed me when I was seventeen.

A smirk covered Emily's face. "I'm not buying it. You're a confident guy who wouldn't let some high school BS define you."

"It didn't define me, Emily." I let out a deep breath. "On the contrary. It's just not worth my time to even think about it."

She nodded slowly and stabbed another calamari. "I'll let you off the hook now because of whom we're sharing our breath with, but I want to know the details at some point."

I smiled, wishing tonight had gone some other way. Now wasn't the moment to confess that I'd been crushing on Emily for the last year, but that was what I'd planned to do.

Her mouth tugged on the side into a deep grin. Yeah, I definitely needed to tell her when there weren't any distractions or the possibility of things going wrong.

And tonight, they could go very wrong.

Emily's phone buzzed, and she groaned. "There had better not be an antique emergency."

She pulled it out of her backpack, and her expression fell.

"What's wrong?" I asked, feeling my pulse quicken.

"It's my Mimi."

Her grandmother on her dad's side, if I remembered correctly.

"What about her? Is she okay?"

Emily looked dazed as she brought her eyes to mine. "She's coming out of surgery. She fell down at her house and needed hip surgery. There's no way my grandpa can take care of her by himself."

"Don't they live here in Seattle?" I asked, seeing the agony wash over Emily's features.

She nodded, texting back. "Yeah. My mom and sister are driving off the ferry now. My dad is stuck with customers at the store. They're going to swing by and pick me up to go visit her." She looked up at me. "If that's okay?"

My stomach clenched. "Of course, it's okay. Why don't you just let me take you? I'll drive you."

She shook her head slowly. "No. I couldn't ask you to do that, and they're already on their way. Mimi is at one of the hospitals on Pill Hill."

"I really don't mind. I'd actually feel better if you let me."

And then I heard her.

Clara's voice bounced off the walls like a ricocheting ball that wouldn't stop.

"Is that you, Lucas Edwards? Lucas? Lucas?" A brief pause. "Lucas."

Emily's gaze caught mine, and she smiled, stuffing her phone into her backpack.

"See? You wouldn't want to miss out on this fun, would you?" She chuckled and gave me a sympathetic smile. "She can have my prawns and linguini."

I dragged my eyes from Emily to see Clara.

It was like time stood still, and not in a good way.

Pieces of Clara's blonde hair curled along her jaw from the messy bob she wore, just like in high school. Her brown eyes locked on mine as her smile grew. She opened up her arms as she made her way over, and it felt like my worst nightmare unfolding right in front of me.

"Don't just stare at her," Emily whispered. "Stand up and hug her. You know she's coming in for it one way or another."

I frowned and shot Emily a look, but she motioned me with her hands to do something.

Emily really had friend-zoned me.

Placing my napkin on the chair next to me, I stood and swept a fake smile across my features as Clara stepped closer.

Clara beamed. "Don't be shy. Come on, Lucas."

"Go on, Lucas," Emily teased as she pulled out her phone from the backpack.

Before I had a chance to escape, Clara wrapped her arms around my neck. "It's so good to see you, Lucas. When Lydia said she ran into you, I hoped I'd be that lucky too."

She took a step back, and I looked at her,

knowing that I should be feeling something.

Anything.

"She said she'd mentioned that I've moved back." Her expression shifted slightly when I didn't answer. "My son wanted to go to school here, so…"

I nodded, pressing my lips into a thin smile.

"My ride is here, Lucas." Emily hopped up and gently squeezed my arm. "I'll talk to you soon, okay?"

Just my luck. The girl I wanted kept me in the friend zone, and the one I couldn't run away from fast enough wanted me.

Here and now.

Before I had the ability to say anything, Emily was out the door.

Chapter Five

Emily

My grandma's frail body didn't match the fiery words coming from her mouth.

"How can a Seattle hospital not have lattes?" She frowned at my grandpa as if he had the answer. "How do they expect me to recover without caffeine?"

"I can run down the street and get you one, Mimi," I offered.

"That's why you're my favorite." She grinned dopily.

Clearly, the meds had taken over. "And what the heck is that contraption doing here? How, in God's name, am I supposed to get up and walk using that thing? It will roll me right onto my ass."

My mom snickered as her mother-in-law's gaze

snapped over to hers.

"What's so funny?" Mimi scowled.

Mimi never swore, so we all knew that whatever was pumping through her veins was doing the talking.

Yeah, this wasn't the crowd I'd be sharing my poetry with.

"You have to use the walker before they let you out of here," my mom explained.

My grandpa nodded and reached for his wife's hand. "Doctor told me so himself."

"Use it, and then what? We have stairs at home."

I knew my parents dreaded this day. My grandparents lived in a mid-century modern that was as flat as a pancake once you got into it. The problem was that the house was perched on one of the steep hillsides that made Seattle famous. There were at least thirty steps just to get into their house.

Mimi always said that was what kept her youthful and looking better than most forty-year-olds.

But now, those steps seemed to be what kept her from going home for a while.

"Just have someone carry me in. Problem

solved." Mimi looked around the room as if she'd figured out world peace.

"I don't think that's a good idea," my mom started, but Mimi ignored her and looked right at me.

I shook my head. "You can't move your leg in certain directions. It could pop out, and all sorts of things could go wrong."

"This is why you need a husband," Mimi said, her eyes sharpening right on me. "Then you could get him to carry me up."

"I'd need two husbands and a stretcher," I pointed out.

Obviously, what my mom just told her went in one ear and out the other.

I chuckled, biting my bottom lip to keep from saying anything.

Mimi's gaze landed on Mae, who'd just opened a bottle of water. "Same goes for you. I don't know what you girls are waiting on. It's not like there's Mr. Perfect out there." Mimi looked at my grandpa. "I got the last perfect model sixty years ago."

Mae touched her chest and smiled, but Mimi

wasn't done. Once she got on a roll about her granddaughters' love lives, it was all over. Mimi was completely the opposite of my other grandma, who'd passed away several years ago. My mom's mom was more... mystic, less forced when it came to love and romance. Mimi was the exact opposite and very blunt, whereas my grandpa was less so. My dad was far more like him than my grandma. How all of these personalities worked out so well was beyond me.

"What you girls need to realize is that in this day and age, you don't look for Mr. Perfect. You pounce on Mr. Good Enough." Mimi scowled at me.

Mae nearly spat out her water. "Not quite how I see it, Mimi."

My mom shook her head. "What we need to do is come up with a plan for your recovery that doesn't involve marrying off your granddaughters to men who can carry you up your stairs."

Mimi chuckled and hiccupped.

Her male nurse strode in with some medicine. He was at least six feet tall, muscular, and totally Mae's type.

"You're single, aren't you?" Mimi asked her nurse.

"Now, Mimi…" The nurse winked at my grandpa. "I told you once already that you're too young for me."

Mimi giggled and scanned the room. "Fifty-five isn't too young for you, but I am happily married."

We all exchanged looks.

Fifty-five? How'd she shave off thirty years? And he has her chart.

The nurse scanned her wristband and asked her for her name and birthday as we all stared at one another in confusion. She was definitely medicated if she was trying to impress the nurse.

"How about dating one of my granddaughters, then?" she pressed.

"Mimi, tell me how you have two ravishing granddaughters my age when you're only fifty-five. Didn't you skip a generation?"

My mom stifled a laugh as Mimi blushed, and my grandpa grinned.

"All I'm saying is they're single and ready to

mingle," Mimi tried again.

"Mimi, we're not." My cheeks reddened when the nurse looked over at me sympathetically and whispered a quick apology while mouthing the word *meds*.

"Where's that latte?" Mimi asked, and I pushed myself off the wall.

"I'll go get it. I saw a Starbucks down the street."

The nurse spun around. "Actually, we have an amazing coffee shop downstairs."

"No way," Mae said, looking immediately interested. Her dream had always been to open a coffee shop, and on Monday, that dream was officially coming true. Her coffee shop was next door to the antique store with an opening between the two. It should have opened months ago, but as with most construction projects, there were… incidents. "I'll come with you."

"Maybe see if they have anything to forage?" my mom suggested. "I haven't eaten all day."

"Why didn't you have dinner?" Mimi asked my mom. Her eyes were getting heavy from whatever medicine the nurse gave her.

"Well, when a call comes in that my mother-in-law has been rushed into surgery, I don't really have time for a meal." My mom chuckled.

Mimi closed her eyes. "Hogwash. There's always time for a meal."

She blinked them open and turned to me. "What about you two? Did you eat?"

Mae shook her head.

"I had some calamari," I answered, which I immediately knew was a mistake.

"Oooh, fancy." Mimi's brows rose.

"She was on a date." Mae flashed a wicked grin in my direction.

"It wasn't a date. It was just dinner with a friend," I assured everyone staring at me.

The nurse laughed, handing Mimi the call button, and made his way out of the room.

"Seriously, you two. He's young and handsome. Why not flirt a little with him?" Mimi looked perplexed. "Does your generation not understand how to flirt?"

The door opened, and Amelia rushed in with James and little Henry right behind her.

He was James's little boy, and he happened to be the cutest one I'd ever seen.

"How's Mimi doing?" Amelia asked me.

Mimi chuckled and shook her head, answering, "Mimi is doing *just* fine."

"She's either Superwoman, or the drugs they've given her are spectacular," I explained to my sister. "She's trying to set us up with the nurse."

"Both of you? That ought to make him happy." James laughed and looked around the room. "Where's Lucas?"

"Oh, I told him he didn't have to come with me. There were some of his old high school friends at the restaurant, and I thought he could catch up with them."

James and Amelia glanced at each other as if they were trading secrets.

And *that*...

That was what I wanted in a relationship. Those moments when you didn't need to say anything, you could just read one other's minds. Kind of like how I felt when reading. The pages and I shared a special something as the words flowed through me and the stories came to life. I could see that same unspoken thing happen between Amelia and James.

"We're just headed down to get Mimi a latte," I told my sister.

"Great. I'll come with you," Amelia said, reaching for my hand to tug me out of the room. "Audrey was going to come with us, but a big group of customers came into the store, so she's helping Dad."

"Don't forget some food," my mom called after us.

When we'd made it the bank of elevators, Amelia stared at me. "So, how'd it go?"

"How'd what go?" I asked. "The reading? It was great."

"No, what James told you. How do you feel about it?"

"Feel about what?" I shook my head.

Amelia's eyes widened. "Oh, nothing. I thought that…" She scowled and pressed the elevator button. "Never mind what I thought. I probably got something confused."

I narrowed my eyes at her as the elevator opened

and we stepped inside. "Okay, what aren't you telling me?"

"Nothing. I don't know a thing about a thing." She shook her head, her dark hair falling around her expression.

Mae whistled. "Uh-oh. Somebody stepped in a big pile of it."

The elevator chimed and spilled us into the bustling hospital lobby. "The nurse said it was on the first floor."

Mae scanned one hallway while I looked down the other to see a huge gift shop.

"Found it." Amelia clapped her hands and pointed.

"How did I not see that when I got here?" I chuckled.

The coffee shop didn't look like a typical hospital café. It looked like an upscale roasting house, complete with velour-covered benches and a nook with books.

"What a fantastic idea." Mae snapped her fingers. "I'm adding that to mine. Why did I not think about having a reading corner?"

I chuckled. "It was meant to be. Mimi broke a hip so you could make your coffeehouse even better."

My sisters laughed as we stepped inside.

"Do you think you're going to reach Monday's deadline?" I asked.

"We already have the permit to open. It's just about making all the things perfect," she explained. "But I've already ordered the food for the grand opening, so yeah. It's happening on Monday, broken hip be damned."

"I'm so excited for you." I hugged Mae as Amelia ordered Mom's drink and one of her own. I scanned the sandwiches and pastries and ordered an assortment to take back upstairs. I'd be surprised if Grandpa had eaten much at all, either.

As we waited for the drinks, I caught Amelia's gaze. "So, spill the beans. What do you know that I don't know?"

"Nothing." She shook her head. "I just thought today was a special day because of the signing and dinner. That's all."

"Well, I think it would have gone a different

direction had he not run into someone from high school. Actually, I don't think it was her that bothered him because I think that's how he got the tickets, but she'd brought up some girl from high school named Clara, and I swear to you, the color drained out of Lucas's face." I shrugged as the drinks were called. "And then he seemed to recover, but where we went for dinner also happened to be the place that the old high school bunch met up for drinks. And who was there? Clara."

"And he wanted to stay back with them while you came here to visit your grandma?" Amelia looked perturbed.

We all wandered over to pick up the two trays of drinks and food to take upstairs. "No. He didn't want to stay at all, but I kind of forced him to. Mom and Mae were already picking me up, and our dinner hadn't even been served yet, and the Clara lady looked extremely happy to see him. It just made sense."

"Did he seem happy to see her?" Amelia asked.

I shook my head. "No, I'd say he was just indifferent. Anyway, I don't know how tonight would have ended had his high school years not come back to haunt him." I chuckled. "Who knows? Maybe I would have confessed my love for him."

Mae and Amelia exchanged looks.

"Guys, I'm kidding." I pushed the elevator button with my pinky as I balanced the tray of drinks.

"You do like him, though, right?" Mae asked.

I nodded. "He's the best friend I could have ever asked for, and a complete surprise at that." I didn't want to tell them that every time I was around him, my stomach dropped, I felt dizzy, and my toes curled just from feeling his breath on my cheek.

Mae frowned. "Come on. Don't you think he's cute?"

My heart fluttered just thinking about him. "I have never hidden my thoughts on the matter. Lucas is a gorgeous guy with a heart of gold. He's just not... boyfriend material. He's told me so, and he's shown me so by going out on dates all the time. Do you realize that on most Friday and Saturday nights, he has a date? The only time he doesn't is when he's babysitting little Henry with me. That does not scream 'settling-down type'."

We walked onto the elevator, and I turned to my

sisters as Amelia pushed the button. "I don't want to lose an amazing friendship because I didn't notice the red flags. And you know me. I fall way too hard. I can't risk it. Lucas is a great friend but a lousy boyfriend, from the looks of it."

I felt kind of bad for not telling my sisters about the poetry residency since I wouldn't be able to help at the store for three months. But I also knew it would be like winning the lottery if it actually happened.

Amelia smiled and shook her head. "I just don't want you to miss out on something that could be spectacular because you're worried about getting hurt."

Kind of like my poetry. My heart screamed at me to fill out the forms and send my samples.

"What I have with him is already spectacular," I murmured, swallowing down the thoughts from earlier. When Clara's gaze landed on Lucas, it was like her incomplete puzzle had found its missing piece. I knew that all it would take was even a minor hint of interest from Lucas, and she'd be all over him.

And I didn't like that feeling one bit, but I had no control over any of it.

Maybe that was why I wanted to leave so quickly. I didn't want to see what could happen tonight between them.

I pushed down the nagging sensation that maybe this woman was different. Maybe the other girls didn't matter, but what if Clara did?

No.

I'd made a conscious effort to shut off thoughts of him with other women. With Lucas, I compartmentalized each aspect of our relationship so that I didn't tumble down a hazardous hill of regret and worry.

I would do that with Clara.

But an ache weighed heavily in my chest.

Lucas was an incredible friend, and I appreciated him.

Like this afternoon...

Lucas's action to go to all that trouble of planning this event and getting tickets, just for me.

But I knew it came through the lens of friendship, and it was vital for me to not let the murky waters of his dating life cast a veil over our interactions and pretend we could be more.

Clara popped into my head again, and I swallowed down my worry as the elevator opened on our floor.

We walked into Mimi's room, and Henry was sitting on his dad's lap as my mom and grandpa whispered not to wake up Mimi.

James smiled at my sister, and they traded that loving look that made me warm up inside. One day, I'd love to share that feeling with someone. My mom hopped up and grabbed the drink tray from me as we quietly spread the drinks and snacks along the window sill as James's phone dinged.

He looked down and bit his lip and shook his head before showing his screen to Amelia. Her expression changed, and she shrugged at him before glancing over at me.

The text had to have been Lucas, and honestly, I had no right to get involved in his personal life.

Chapter Six

Lucas

Clara ran her fingers through her short blonde hair and took a step back, glancing at Emily as she left. I sat back down at the table, wishing I'd gone with Emily.

"Is that your girlfriend?" Clara asked.

It was none of her business.

I brought my gaze back to Clara.

"No."

She let out a dramatic sigh and touched her chest as she slid into Emily's empty chair.

"Thank goodness." She smiled and brought her eyes to mine. "I haven't known how to reach out to you."

"Why would you?" I asked as the server brought our dinner over.

Before he could put Emily's plate down, I held

up my hand. "Would you mind putting that in a to-go box?"

The server nodded and went back to the kitchen as I picked up my fork and took a bite of asparagus.

"Well, a lot of time has passed. You know, it's not like we're getting any younger." She kept her eyes on mine. Her gaze was unsettling.

Most men would probably find her attractive, but I knew what she was capable of and wanted no part of any of it.

I just wanted Emily, and I'd let her leave.

Out the door.

Without telling her how I really felt.

"So, what have you been up to all these years, Lucas?"

"Not much," I said, bringing my eyes to hers as I cut my steak.

This girl wasn't good at reading body language.

"Listen, I've wanted to apologize for a really long time, but…" She pursed her lips together. "But it just never seemed adequate over a phone call or a message."

I nodded, feeling my stomach tighten into knots. "It's really not a big deal. It all happened a long time ago. We were kids."

"I should have known better." She shook her head. "It was really wrong of me, but maybe on some level, I'd wanted it to be you."

"I don't really know what to say." So, I took a bite of steak and calculated how many bites I could take to polish it off.

"Hear me out. I know it sounds crazy, but maybe we can go out sometime." She glanced at the group over at the bar. "I'm an empty nester soon, and I'll have plenty of free time. Maybe I could prove to you how much I've changed."

I nodded, watching Clara's smile widen as she mistook my silence as acceptance. She slid her hands over her messy bob and shrugged. "What do you think? Can we at least meet for coffee?"

The server brought over Emily's meal as I traded him for my credit card and forked in a few pieces of my steak.

"Uh, yeah. I don't know, Clara. I'm really pretty

full up on life right now." I shook my head, chewing.

If I could be any more obnoxious, I'd be surprised.

Yet, Clara just stared at me like some lost puppy dog.

"I just don't think it's a coincidence that after a decade and a half, you reached out to my best friend for some tickets at the same time I moved back to Seattle." She tilted her chin and let out a sigh.

I just took another bite of steak, wishing every second that I was sitting next to Emily.

"Well, maybe I'll bump into you at some point," she offered. "I mean, we had something in common all those years ago. Maybe it's still there."

"Teenage hormones." I studied her closely, noticing the stress lines in her brow, the frown lines along her lips, the weariness in her eyes. Things hadn't been easy for Clara.

But that wasn't my doing.

"That's what we had in common. I don't want to give you the wrong impression, Clara. I'm not interested." I shook my head. "I'm kind of tied up right now with someone else."

"But you told Lydia you were single."

"It's complicated."

She scowled at me. "What? Were you only single until you saw something you didn't like about me?"

"Not at all," I said softly. "I'm sure you're a lovely person."

I stood up. "But I'm just not the guy you used to know."

The server brought over plastic utensils and the receipt that I quickly signed. Clara reached for the full bottle of wine and laughed. "I guess you won't be needing this, then."

I smiled, shoving the plastic fork into my back pocket. "Guess not."

She stood and came over to hug me again. This time, I picked up the heavy scents of liquor and stale perfume.

A few years ago, I might have taken advantage of the situation. Who knew? Maybe it would have even gone somewhere.

But not tonight.

Not now.

There was only one woman I wanted.

"Enjoy the wine, and maybe I'll see you around. Welcome back to Seattle."

She nodded, clutching the wine bottle before she turned around and made her way back to everyone waiting for her.

As I reached the door, I heard a wave of laughter and couldn't wait to get out of the restaurant.

I couldn't believe how in less than twelve hours, my entire life plan got sidelined, elbowed, and stepped on by some crap from high school.

This morning felt so amazing. I knew I was about to confess to the woman I was falling for that I wanted to try something more with her.

And before the night was through, an ex who'd colored my view of women jumped into the picture and screwed up the entire night.

But I was a glutton for punishment.

I needed to see Emily again. Besides, she needed to eat.

As I texted James on the way to my car, I thought

about how crazy it was that my high school girlfriend showed up on the very night I needed things to go right.

I didn't ask for much in life.

But why, tonight, did things go sideways?

I found my car and drove through the busy Seattle streets, turning onto the hill that housed several medical clinics and hospitals, and turned into a parking garage.

It was as if the world decided to give me a break as I spotted a parking spot right next to the elevator. Turning off the ignition, I grabbed her dinner and nearly hopped out of the car.

Maybe all wasn't lost.

James had texted me the floor Mimi was on, and I made my way onto the parking garage elevator. The faint smells of grease and someone's leftover perfume filled my nostrils. It was a sickly sweet, mechanical smell, and for some reason, it brought back the thought of Clara.

Great.

A woman I hadn't thought about in a decade was suddenly being forced into my mind. I rolled my eyes at the annoyance of it all as the elevator doors opened, and I quickly spotted the next bank of elevators leading to patients' rooms.

The old perfume and grease smells traded for the sterile air of the hospital. I rushed into the gift shop, found a pretty bouquet, and paid quickly before making my way to the elevators. Several people stepped into the carriage with me, and one of the women turned around and smiled.

"That smells heavenly. I love garlic." She smiled.

I shook my head when she glanced at my takeout box, not the flowers. Laughing, I nodded. "I forgot I had food with me. Sorry. It's been a day."

"Aren't they all like that?" She chuckled as the doors opened, and we all spilled onto the hospital floor. The group went to the left, and I spotted the room number signs leading to Mimi's.

I heard my cousin's laughter and knew I was headed in the right direction. It was crazy to me. Even in a hospital room, they could sound like one big, happy family. More laughter rang into the hallway as I looked at the nurses' station across from Mimi's room. I could see why James felt like he'd won the lottery with Amelia. Her family was incredible.

It was different from mine but in a good way.

The nurses saw me as I pointed at the hospital room with all the ruckus, and they nodded.

The moment I stepped inside, I felt the love oozing from every part of the room. Emily's grandpa held Mimi's hand as she smiled, looking lovingly at her daughter-in-law, while James and Amelia sat in the corner with Henry and Mae. Their eyes met mine, and James smiled, but I didn't see Emily anywhere.

"I'm sorry to hear about your accident," I told Mimi as she brought her gaze to the flowers. I set them on the rolling table next to her.

"Lucas, you're too sweet. Do you realize you're the only one who brought me flowers?" Mimi eyed the rest of them, and I chuckled. "You'd make an excellent grandson-in-law."

Emily's mom laughed and shook her head, looking at James. "It's the meds. You're doing just fine as an almost son-in-law."

I waggled my brows at my cousin, and he

laughed as Mimi breathed in the scent of the flowers.

"Hey, stranger," Emily's sweet voice sang behind me.

I spun around to see Emily standing with a bag of chips.

"I brought you dinner," I said, feeling every part of my body pull to her.

Her smile lit up, and she swept a quick kiss on my cheek. "You're the best. I was literally swimming in regret over leaving the prawns behind. These chips just weren't cutting it."

She took the box from me as I spun around to have Mimi's eyes right on me. "Emily, he brought me flowers. Isn't that sweet of him?"

"Very." Emily nodded, opening up the takeout box. "He's just full of surprises, but no fork."

I laughed and reached behind me. "That's where you're wrong." I pulled out the plastic fork from the restaurant and held it for her to grab.

She quickly peeled off the plastic wrap and smiled. "Hmm. You think of everything."

"So, how long have you two been friends?" Mimi

questioned, eyeing her granddaughter.

Emily forked in a mouthful of pasta and left me to answer. "About a year, almost as long as they've been dating." I pointed at my cousin.

She nodded. "Why aren't you two an item?"

"She's just not that into me," I teased, and Emily nearly choked on her linguini.

I patted her back, and she nodded, swallowing. "He's not the settling-down type, Mimi."

"Is that so?" Mimi chuckled, sounding almost melodic. She looked a little dopey, so I was pretty sure it was the drugs pumping through her for pain. "Maybe he hasn't met the right woman yet."

I laughed, rocking back on my heels. "Or I might have, and she's just not interested."

Mimi looked perplexed, nestled her head back on the pillow, and was out like a light.

"The nurse just loaded her up again," Emily explained. "She did a mini-nap right before you got here, woke up, drank a latte, and bam."

"So, what's the prognosis?" I asked. "Did the surgery go well?"

"Funny you should ask," Emily's mom said, laughing. "We just had someone from PT come and talk to us while Emily was getting some chips."

"Yeah?" Emily asked, surprised.

"And they have a therapist on Marigold Island who can work with her." Her mom glanced at her grandpa.

"She's not going to be happy about living at your house, Mom." Emily grimaced, glancing at Mae and Amelia. "And your bathrooms with a shower are on the second level."

"That's true," her grandpa agreed.

"I have a spare bedroom. My bungalow would be perfect. How long is it for?" Emily asked, glancing at her grandparents, even though one was out like a light. "Mom would drive Mimi nuts with all of her rules, and I don't have any, so…"

Her grandpa chuckled. "That might make it hurt less, for sure. Mimi hates rules."

She nodded in agreement. "Me too. So, it's settled. Mimi and Grandpa will stay at my house for the next six weeks, give or take."

"Are you sure, sweetie? Mimi can be a bit of a handful." My mom bit her bottom lip and eyed Mae and Amelia. "Would you girls chip in if she needed help?"

"Of course, Mom." Mae nodded.

"I can help too," I offered. "It's not like my schedule is packed lately."

Emily smiled, her eyes connecting with mine briefly before she nodded. "I've noticed that, but on this note, I should get out of here so I can start organizing a place for them in the spare room."

"I can take you back," I offered.

"You don't live on Marigold." She shook her head. "I'll just…"

Mimi's eyes popped open. "Just let the man give you a ride, Emily."

Chapter Seven

Emily

The ferry ride over to Marigold Island last night had to have been the weirdest one ever. I wanted to question Lucas about Clara, but every time I went to ask, it was like he intuitively knew and switched the subject before it ever began.

We spoke a lot about my poetry, and I even promised I'd share with him the poems I'd sent in with the application.

And I was so happily full on my linguine that I didn't fight it and let myself rest on the way back to Marigold. I knew I had a lot of work ahead of me to get ready for Mimi and Grandpa to show up, so silence mostly sat between us.

But I couldn't shake the feeling that something

was off.

Was it because I'd mentioned the residency?

When he'd dropped me off at my house, he insisted on walking me up to my doorstep because he always did. And it was like the air between us was electrified even more, but he said goodnight, and I went inside.

The silence amplified the nagging thoughts I'd had about Lucas and Clara, so I pumped up the stereo last night and spent the entire night organizing the spare bedroom and wondering if I had merely imagined the hyped-up tension between us.

But what I knew I needed this morning more than anything was a sausage and cheese biscuit from Milo's. That was the only thing that would get me through the busy day working at Baubles and Curiosities before heading back home to clean.

Rick wandered out to the counter that looked particularly cheery in the morning sunlight. I usually frequented the place on Friday nights when the lights were dim, music played, and people filled the bar.

"Hey, I missed you last night," Rick said,

smiling.

I slid onto the stool and let out an exasperated sigh before collapsing my head into my hands. "It's been a crazy twenty-four hours." I looked back up to see him watching me, concerned.

"Anything I can do to help?"

I shook my head. "No. It's just a lot. I had a great day seeing my favorite mystery writer with one of my best friends, and then my evening ended with a call that my grandma broke her hip."

"Oh, no. Mimi?"

I chuckled, nodding. "Oh, yeah. You know her."

"After last year's Christmas party, I think the entire island knows her."

"Truer words, my friend. Mimi got a little frisky on the eggnog. I didn't know things could jiggle like that." I grimaced.

"It gave me hope for being seventy." Rick laughed, shaking his head.

"Actually, she's eighty."

His eyes widened. "I'm sure she won't let her hip slow her down any." Rick smiled, inputting my breakfast order. "Well, I want you to know your presence was missed last night."

"Even though I sit in the corner reading my book all night?"

He nodded. "Especially because of that. You're a staple for this place."

I laughed. "Great. Soon, you can start selling tickets."

"I'm not above it." He shrugged. "Did you need any help?"

"With what?"

"Getting your grandparents settled at your house."

His offer surprised me, but it shouldn't. Everyone around Marigold Island offered a hand when needed, but this offer felt…

Different.

I smiled, glancing around the bar. "Thanks. I just might take you up on that. Milo's looks really different in the day. Not so moody. Kind of like you."

He chuckled and shook his head. "You think I look moody?"

"Maybe brooding with your tattoos and dark eyes."

"Boy, you do read a lot."

"What can I say?" I smiled, feeling his gaze on me a few seconds longer than usual. Maybe Amelia was right about Rick. Maybe he actually had a thing for me. "I even write a little poetry."

"You do?"

It felt freeing to admit that there was something I enjoyed. I could scream to strangers what I loved to do, but I clammed up the moment I thought about my family.

But I could tell Lucas, and for that, I was very grateful.

"I'd love to hear it sometime."

"Yeah? Really?"

"Totally." He tapped the counter. "Okay. I'll go grab your order. I threw in a hashbrown patty."

"You're the best." I grinned, hopping off the stool as he wandered toward the kitchen where my breakfast awaited.

I snatched the bag from Rick and smiled before spinning around and wandering out the door.

It might be kind of cool if I got the residency. I wouldn't just be the Evans girl who works at Baubles and Curiosities. I'd be the poet who worked at Baubles and Curiosities. The thought made me chuckle as I waved goodbye.

The morning sunshine sprinkled its rays on my bare skin as I walked onto the sidewalk. This was one of the many things I loved about living on Marigold Island. I could park my car in one area of town and wander to the other without much trouble.

But there was no doubt our little island was growing and becoming more and more of a tourist destination, which was definitely good for our family business, and it would do wonders for Mae's new coffee shop.

The sidewalks on both sides of the street were filled with boutiques, cafés, a salon, galleries, and a couple of breweries. The town had large planters cemented to every other door that overflowed this time of year with geraniums, phlox, and petunias. Dark green benches scattered the sidewalks to give people a place to rest and regroup before moving on to more shopping.

Our little island was definitely planning for the future.

The sweet smell of spring mingled with the salty air of the ocean, and I knew there was nowhere else I'd rather be.

A familiar whistle from behind made me stop in my tracks.

"Bryce, one day you're going to whistle at the wrong girl and get your lights punched out." I spun around to see Bryce and his toothless Doberman, Herman, walking down the sidewalk toward us. My sisters and I had gone to school with him starting in grade school, and to say we knew some unsavory secrets about him was putting it mildly. He was like an extra brother who had a dirty old grandpa's mind.

Bryce laughed and shook his head. "Sorry. I thought that paper bag was Dottie."

"Oh, right. You always have to whistle at poor Dottie on Herman's behalf." I exaggerated a wink and laughed.

"Those are the rules. I didn't make them, but Herman has a serious crush on that pug."

"Story of her life." I snickered, holding up my

bag. "But nope. It's not Dottie. Just my breakfast."

"Ah, biscuit sandwich from Milo's?"

I nodded.

"You know, he's got a thing for you." Bryce said, glancing behind him toward the bar.

"Don't go spreading island rumors," I scolded him.

"Just sayin' what I know." He beamed, walking side by side with me. "He looks forward to your reading at his bar every Friday night."

I rolled my eyes as we made it to the corner.

"Whatever you say, pot-stirrer."

Bryce chuckled and waved goodbye. Every morning, without fail, Bryce walked Herman to the post office. They took off down the road while I waited for a car to go by and crossed at the crosswalk.

By the time I got to the store, Audrey opened the door to let me in. "You look really tired, Emily. You okay?"

I yawned, setting my bag down on a counter. "I think I stayed up too late trying to get things ready for Mimi and Grandpa."

My sister sucked in a breath before pursing her lips together into a grimace. "Yeah. I heard about your offer to let them move in. Brave soul." She patted my shoulder.

"I also remember something about Mom telling me all my sisters would help," I teased.

She grinned. "Of course I will. Totally. Of course. You can count on me. Always."

I laughed, pulling out the breakfast sandwich and handing her the hashbrown.

"What if they don't move out?" my sister asked.

"Then I guess that means you'll be getting a new roommate." I chuckled, taking a bite of the sandwich.

Mae wandered through the entrance between her coffee shop and the antique store and waved.

"Good morning, Emily. How did everything go with Lucas after you left?"

"Uh… fine. Like usual. Why?" I cocked my head, taking another bite.

Why wouldn't it have gone well? It wasn't like we didn't hang out all the time. And then it hit me. Maybe she knew something about Lucas and Clara.

"Just wondered." She shrugged, glancing at my half-eaten breakfast sandwich. "Hey, she got a hash brown." She pointed at Amelia and then at me. "And you got a sandwich? What about me? The older sister?"

"That's what happens when you jump ship and open your new place. Besides, soon, I'll be ordering pastries and muffins from you."

Mae pointed at the entrance between the two. "Just right between there." She could barely contain the excitement. I was so happy for her.

A few customers came in as I polished off the sandwich and threw away the bag, and Audrey went to help them.

Mae wandered back to her coffee shop and locked the door between the two buildings while I propped my bag behind the counter. I'd take it upstairs in a few minutes.

I thought back to what Bryce said about Rick. Was that true? Sure, he'd asked me out a couple of times, but it wasn't really…

Actually, he had asked me out a few times, and he probably meant it.

I was so dense.

Maybe he *did* like me.

But I didn't exactly feel that way toward him, and sure, he was super good-looking, but I didn't get any butterflies or zaps of electricity.

Looking at him was like looking at most men.

Zippo.

Unlike Lucas.

All it took was a brush of a hand or a glance, and I was a goner for my best friend.

Which led me back to submitting to the poetry residency. The time apart would probably be a good thing, so I could get my head screwed back on straight and quit lusting over something I couldn't have and shouldn't have. He might even make it easy for me and find someone while I was away.

The thought felt like a hot rock in the bottom of my belly, and I scowled.

Audrey walked over and waved her hand in front of my face. "Yoohoo. Anyone in there?"

"Oh, sorry. I was just thinking about something."

"I'm sure Mimi won't care whether your house is

spotless. Don't stress about it."

"Yeah. No. You're totally right." I nodded, thankful she didn't know what I was really thinking about.

The bell dinged as the door opened, and I glanced to see Rick coming inside. I waved when he spotted me, and he made his way over.

"Hey, Emily." His voice sounded more gruff than usual. "I realized that I offered to help you with Mimi, but I didn't give you my number."

Audrey couldn't wipe the smile off her face as Amelia wandered over, holding a stack of books.

"Hey, Rick. What's up?" she asked, glancing at me before standing next to him.

"Emily mentioned your grandparents will be living with her for a few weeks, and I wanted to help her out any way I could."

Amelia's brows rose. "Oh, yeah? That's sweet."

I frowned at my sister and eyed toward the bookshelf, hoping she'd take her stack of books and nosy self that way.

"Oh, thanks." I reached down to my backpack

and pulled out my phone. "That's really sweet, like my sister said."

"Ah, no problem at all." He started reciting his number as the bell dinged again, but this time, Lucas walked into the store.

He instantly spotted me and smiled as he walked toward me.

My heart skipped a beat, but not for the usual reason when seeing Lucas. I tried not to smile when I realized two worlds were about to collide.

Never in a million years would something like this happen to me.

Rick gave me the last digit as Lucas arrived and glanced at me.

"Thanks, Rick. It's beyond kind of you to offer help." I nodded, sliding my phone into the back pocket of my jeans.

"Oh, this is Rick?" Lucas asked, his eyes widening.

Rick nodded and looked over at me before looking at Lucas.

"Yeah. He's the one who got me addicted to

garlic fries while reading."

Lucas smiled, nodding. "I've heard of those. They're a big hit."

"It's the fresh-cut fries." He smiled and nodded. "You're Lucas, right? Part of the Edwards family? The one that owns the orchard and beverage company?"

"Yeah. That's me." Lucas nodded, tilting his chin slightly as if he were trying to put the pieces of the puzzle together. "So, you offered to help…"

"Oh, I just offered to lend a hand to get her grandparents situated. She mentioned it to me earlier this morning."

Lucas's brows quirked. "This morning?"

I couldn't help but smile. "Yup. This morning."

"Alright. I'd better get back. I just didn't want you to think I was a man who'd go back on my word."

I chuckled and shook my head. "I'd never think that, Rick. Thanks again."

Lucas watched Rick walk out of the store before turning to me with a wide grin.

"Is that the Rick you have a crush on?"

I stomped my foot. "I do *not* have a crush on

him."

Lucas's grin only widened. "Your sister thinks otherwise."

I shrugged and leaned against the counter. "Why? Does it matter?"

"Nah. Just trying to figure things out with you. That's all."

I hugged myself, kind of liking the rise I was getting out of Lucas. "I'm an open book."

"Yeah? Are you gonna call Rick for help?"

"Beats me. Depends how things go tonight."

"Why? Are you meeting him tonight or something?"

I rolled my eyes and gently swatted at him. "No, silly. I mean at my house, cleaning up. If I don't get as much done tonight, maybe I will ask for help."

"Don't forget I offered too. Technically, I offered first."

"Yeah, but you don't live here. He does."

He nodded as silence sat between us. There'd been a shift since last night, and I honestly couldn't tell what it was from.

My skin still buzzed just from his being around me, and I couldn't help but get all warm and fuzzy standing next to him, but I...

I just didn't know what had changed.

Unless it was Clara.

"And wait a second. What are you doing here, anyway?"

Lucas took a step closer, and I immediately felt a charge run through me. Even my fingernails felt like they were sizzling. I looked away quickly and drew a hidden breath, praying he didn't see how he could affect me, especially with Clara in the picture.

"I told you I wanted to help you, and I knew if I wasn't on the island, you wouldn't ask for help." He shrugged, giving me the cute little quirky smile that always turned me on... in a completely platonic way. "I just didn't know you had a line of men begging to help."

"You can't stay at my house," I blurted out, and he laughed.

"I wasn't planning on it. My parents are in Portugal, so I'm going to stay at the orchard."

"Oh, right. That makes sense." Not being

accustomed to having houses all over the place, I always forgot that Lucas and his family did. They collect houses like some people collect postage stamps.

"Thank you. That's really nice of you."

"And I was hoping we could chat later." His voice lowered. "It's important."

"About what?" I asked, already knowing the answer.

"Our friendship."

Yup, it was Clara.

"Fine. I'm off at four o'clock. I'll meet you at my house."

Chapter Eight

Lucas

Great. Emily did have a crush on Rick. They were trading numbers, and I'd obviously interrupted them.

Maybe when her sister name-dropped Rick, that had been her sister's way of warning me, but I was too stubborn to listen. But at least I found out now and not after I poured my heart out, only to have her reject me.

My knee bobbed up and down as I sat at my laptop and sent a few emails about a property that was getting renovated. I'd recently bought a small apartment complex on the outskirts of Seattle, and it needed to be completely rehabbed. I think the technical term for the previous owner was slumlord, and I certainly wasn't going to let that continue.

It was one of the few things I excelled at besides being the fun uncle. My family had been lucky in the beverage industry, and my grandparents had built an amazing business. But there was no denying that once my cousin took over, the company grew in all ways.

The truth of the matter was that we were all well taken care of, but I never wanted to just sit and twiddle my thumbs. I didn't have the savvy that James had when it came to running the beverage company, and I was fortunate enough to have the means to try things that interested me. So far, I hadn't burned through any of my inheritance, and I planned on keeping it that way.

My phone buzzed, and I saw Nina, my sister, appear on the screen. I answered it on speaker, and she groaned.

"You weren't supposed to pick up. I wanted to leave you a message."

I chuckled. "Do you want me to hang up and we try this again?"

She laughed. "No, but here's the news. Mom and Dad are coming home early from their trip. They decided they want to celebrate their anniversary by renewing their vows."

"Okay. That's different for them."

"Anyway, I'm supposed to tell you that two weeks from Saturday is theirs and to find a date. Mom has all kinds of fantasies about her and Dad dancing with her kids."

I groaned, sliding my head into my hands. "Can't we just dance together?"

"Ew. No. You're my brother. Like it's hard for you to find a date. Why not bring Emily? Mom and Dad love her."

"I think she's interested in someone, and I don't want screw that up."

She fell silent and cleared her throat. "Weren't you kind of into her?"

I laughed. "Not just kinda, but yeah... I... I don't want to get in the way of whatever it is she wants, and she's made it pretty clear that I'll forever be in the friend zone."

"This doesn't sound like my brother."

"I met the guy she's into this morning, so it made things pretty clear."

"Well, things change. Don't give up. Don't get down. And remember, two Saturdays from now."

"Sounds good. But why couldn't Mom just text me this?"

"They're headed out for one last boat trip and wouldn't have reception."

"Ah, gotcha." I nodded, thinking about my parents.

Their vision of a boat would count as a yacht in most people's world. But that was the thing about my parents. They were sometimes oblivious, quirky, and in their own bubble.

My sister hung up the phone, and I nodded, realizing that was about how most conversations in our family went. They weren't really deep, just surface level.

The only person in my family I'd ever felt like I could have a real conversation with was James. It was probably why we'd become so close when we were young.

To see Emily and her family last night at the hospital, surrounding Mimi and just so close, made me realize what I wanted. I didn't want to have surface-level encounters with my own family. I wanted someone I could share my soul with and confide in, tell them about my dreams, insecurities, hopes…

That person had been Emily.

And it still could be as long as I didn't screw anything up by trying to make us more than what we were supposed to be.

I thought about Rick. He had a good reputation, had a great business, and seemed like a nice guy.

And Emily deserved a nice guy.

But she deserved even more than that.

Just like this poetry gig. She deserved it, and I didn't want to stand in her way.

I tapped my finger on the desk and stared out the window toward the water. My grandparents had left the family a huge orchard with a sprawling home overlooking the ocean, and just recently, we'd started holding festivals on the property again in the fall. Emily was here with me on the last one, and it was almost magical. She probably had more fun bobbing for apples and eating fritters than the kids.

I smiled, thinking back to it.

There was a lot about Marigold Island that I loved, but I'd built my life in Seattle. Suddenly, that didn't seem so appealing.

I let out a deep breath and closed the laptop.

Things were going to be fine. I'd help Emily out however she needed. I'd stay in the friend lane because it was better than no lane at all.

And if it didn't work out between Rick and her, then I'd be there to pick up the pieces.

I glanced at the clock and stood up. It was four o'clock. Time to go tell her the exact opposite from what I'd planned on the way over here.

Grabbing my keys and wallet, I looked around my grandparents' home. The place was like a time capsule with its gaudy and ornate furniture and wallpaper. But it brought a strange sort of comfort.

From the outside looking in, my grandparents might have looked prim and proper, even unemotional.

But I knew how fiercely they loved and how loyal they were when they raised James. It always made me see them a little differently from how others did.

As I walked out to my car, I glanced around the

orchard and took in a deep breath. The air was definitely different here from Seattle. It smelled cleaner, somehow lighter.

By the time I pulled up to Emily's house, I felt better about my decision to let things go. I didn't need to get down on my knees and proclaim my feelings for her. Not after she finally got to the point of exchanging numbers with the guy. And she might not even be around for three months.

I skipped up to the door and rang the doorbell. Within seconds, Emily swung open the door and smiled.

"Right on time." She pulled me in and laughed. "I need your big, bulging muscles to lift a few boxes for me."

I stood in her tiny foyer. "What? No hugs or a smooch or how are you? Just straight to work?"

She stood on her toes and swept a quick kiss on my cheek, hugged me even quicker, and patted my back. "How are you?"

I smiled. "Better now, I suppose."

Her bungalow was perfectly Emily. The foyer was cheery with a small table where she always had flowers and something that smelled good on top. She'd painted the walls a light grey, almost white, but she had a series of tiny wildflower paintings in vivid reds, purples, and blues.

The rest of her house was just as cheery, just like Emily.

"Okay, so I scooted the tables out of the walkway so that Mimi wouldn't crash her walker into them. But for some reason, the small butcherblock island I have won't roll. It's like the wheels are busted."

"I can take a look at it." I nodded.

"And then I have a few boxes to lift out of the guest room."

I laughed. "It went from a couple to a few?"

"I'm tricky like that." Her gaze stayed on mine. "And then we can talk about whatever it is that you wanted to tell me."

"Sounds like a plan," I said, feeling like I'd made the right decision. It was time for me to back off a little, define our friendship a little better.

Because right now, all I wanted to do was bring her into me and kiss her.

I followed her down the short hallway that had photos of her sisters and parents hanging on the walls.

The kitchen looked like a tornado had hit.

"What happened?" I chuckled, taking everything in.

"I realized I'd better sort my pantry and toss the stuff that's out of date. When it's just me, I know better than to eat the four-year-old oat bran, but Mimi and Grandpa probably wouldn't check the dates."

I picked up some Cheerios and rattled the box. "Why don't they move?"

Her cheeks blushed, and she grabbed the box back. "Because it's one solid mass. Apparently, the ocean humidity doesn't do great things year after year." She flipped the lid down on the box. "Because this cereal is from… three years ago."

"I had no idea you had this dirty little secret about you." I glanced down at the table of candy. "I'm guessing I shouldn't trust the gummy worms?"

She shrugged and laughed. "Meh. I have better things to do with my time, like read or dream about seeing the world."

I scooted out a chair and took a seat. "I thought you loved it here."

Emily nodded. "I do, but I'd love to travel and experience new places and things as long as I have Marigold to come home to."

"I get that."

She walked over to the counter and reached for a mug in her cupboard. "Want any coffee?"

"Sure."

She poured me a cup and stared at me over the rim of hers as she drank. Setting it down, she leaned against the counter and crossed her arms.

The jeans showed off her curvy body, and I had to rip my eyes away to remember that I couldn't go there.

"Umm... what you wanted to talk to me about... is it bad?" The tenderness in her voice tore me apart.

"No, not at all." I shook my head, and she pushed herself away from the counter. "I just..."

Her lips quirked into a smile, but I saw worry reflected behind her gaze. "Is it about Clara?"

I frowned and stood. "No way." I shook my head. "Not even."

I caught her letting out a silent breath and nodded. "Emily, I really don't have any interest there with her, and I told her as much."

Her eyes widened. "You did?"

"Yeah." I nodded. "She was coming on kind of strong, and I just didn't want to lead her on. I don't know. Maybe the old me would have jumped at the chance for old time's sake, but there's too much there that I just don't like. She was really selfish back in high school, and I doubt much has changed."

"Are you saying people can't change their ways?" she asked, setting her cup down on the counter.

I had. The moment I met Emily, I knew I didn't care about going out with any other woman again.

But she wouldn't believe it.

Letting out a sigh, my eyes stayed on her. "No, I'm not saying that."

She chuckled, and her head flew back slightly as she smiled. "Except for maybe you. I can't imagine you settling down."

"Maybe you're wrong."

She blinked a couple of times and shook her

head. "No. I don't know of one weekend that you haven't gone out with someone, and that doesn't count the weeknights. It's in your blood. You don't want to miss out on the next best thing, and it's okay. Not everyone is the settling down type."

I never should have pretended to be going on dates when I was actually babysitting Henry. I thought it would be funny the first few times, and then I'd tell her my secret. But every time I'd decided to tell her how I felt, she'd make some snappy remark about my not being boyfriend material.

"And what about you? Do you want to settle down?" I asked, standing from the chair and polishing off my coffee.

Emily turned to the fridge and pulled out two peach sparkling waters. One of the many things we'd bonded over this year. She handed me one and took a sip of hers.

"Absolutely. Once God puts a great guy on my porch with a bow on his head, I'm ready."

I laughed. "So that's what it would take?"

She nodded as I drank some of the water and

looked at her butcher block island. "Where did you want me to roll this?"

"Over to the side so there's more room for Mimi. I think closer to the window."

I bent over, unlocked the wheels, and stood up. "That ought to do it."

"What did you do?" she asked as I easily pushed it toward the window.

"Unlocked the wheels."

She flicked her eyes to the window in annoyance. "I swear I did that."

"Okay, next on your list?"

"Right this way." She motioned for me to follow her down the hall to the bedrooms. She stopped in front of the spare room, which I'd seen a night or two when we'd lived it up a little too much. She'd managed to shove the guest bed into the center of the room, leaving enough room on both sides for her grandparents and Mimi's walker. She'd had the bed shoved to the wall before like a couch. Three boxes teetered on one another.

"They look heavy."

She grinned at me wickedly. "Oh, they are.

They're books. We'll put them in the attic, but I'll need you to help get them down for me when my grandparents leave. I don't want them to get ruined."

"Maybe I ought to help you find a boyfriend," I teased.

"Blech."

"What about that Rick guy?" I asked, trying to sound casual as I hoisted the first box. The box wasn't actually all that heavy.

"He's a nice guy," she said, walking into the hallway.

I followed her as she stopped and reached for a pole that she used to yank down the ladder. Balancing the box on the steps, I made my way into the nearly empty attic and brought the box up.

"I think he might be into me," she said, craning her neck up the stairs. "But I doubt he'd show up to date number two, either."

My jaw clenched at the thought, and I let out a deep breath.

Making my way back down the steps, I hopped onto the floor from the last tread and turned to see her looking as cute as ever as she thought about what she'd just said.

But was she into him? This might be my only chance...

Without thinking, I stepped closer to Emily with her eyes locking on mine. And she smiled, and I knew I needed to kiss her.

Chapter Nine

Emily

Lucas moved a fraction closer to me. The air between us jolted with something new and thrilling with each passing breath. This wasn't how friends behaved. Every part of my body felt charged from the heat behind his gaze.

His gaze.

He'd never looked at me like this before.

I swallowed down my worries as he took another step closer. His hand slowly moved up my spine, cradling my head in his palm.

"Lucas," I whispered, feeling the need growing.

His eyes dipped to my mouth as my breath caught, and I prayed this wasn't a dream.

"Pinch me," I murmured, looking into his gaze.

"How about I kiss you instead?" he said, smiling.

Raw need swirled through me as his gaze darkened with desire.

"What about our friendship?" I asked, feeling my pulse rise.

He pressed his forehead against mine and let out a steady breath, keeping his gaze locked on mine.

"You're my best friend, Emily. That won't change." The gruffness in his voice caught me off-guard and turned me on even more.

The thought of his lips elsewhere heated my body to insane temps as I searched his eyes for answers.

"That won't change," he repeated quietly as his lips met mine.

Closing my eyes, I felt the softness of his mouth caress mine as his fingers twisted through my hair.

Even in my wildest dreams, and I'd had plenty, the dreamed kiss between us wasn't as powerful as this felt. His breath changed as I leaned into him, feeling his firmness dig into me.

He looped his arms around me and pressed me against the wall in the hallway. His mouth nipped at my lips as he cupped both of my hands in his, raising them above my head.

Lucas's mouth slowly moved to my neck. His breath skittered across my skin as I breathed in slowly, feeling every brush of his lips and the heat of his breath.

"Lucas," I whispered, opening my eyes to see him caging me in with one arm while his other stayed above us, cupping my hands. "I…"

His mouth came down to mine, harder this time.

I parted my lips, inviting him in as my heart raced with something I didn't even understand. The peach of the seltzer mingled with my breath as he let out a little groan, moving his mouth away.

"You taste so good," he said softly as my eyes fluttered open to reveal my best friend.

The guy I'd wanted from the beginning.

But I was scared.

He let go of my hands and softly swiped his thumb across my lips before kissing me again.

If he took me to my bedroom, I knew I wouldn't be able to resist.

And there was a really big part of me that hoped

he'd do that.

He dropped his hands and gripped my hips, pulling me even closer to him as our kisses turned needy.

My hands roamed under his shirt. Feeling his hard abs under the fabric made me nearly delirious.

This wasn't happening.

Was it?

The heat coursing through my veins melted away every worry I'd had about Lucas breaking my heart, replacing them with nothing more than a restless want. His tongue flicked against mine, and I let out a little moan.

His mouth broke from mine, and he took a step back, resting his arm against the wall again as if I weren't the only one who needed to be braced.

Lucas's gaze burned into me as I bit my lip, silently begging for more.

"That's how I feel about you, Emily." He closed his eyes and let out a deep breath. "And that's what I'd planned on telling you at dinner the other night, but…"

"But life?" I asked, still feeling breathless and charged with something that scared me.

He nodded, still leaning toward me. "I know you don't think I'm boyfriend material, but I've changed."

That kiss disarmed me completely.

Usually, I would have been able to come up with something snappy to say and put him in his place.

Friend zone him for the safety of my heart.

But as I looked into his eyes, I could see the rawness and vulnerability, and the connection between us had been a shockwave to my system.

When I looked at him, all I wanted to do was write poetry.

Right... I might be leaving for three months.

"I don't know what to say," I said, feeling my cheeks flush with longing.

He straightened up and nodded. "When I saw you with Rick today, I knew I needed to let the idea of you go. That was what I was going to tell you. That I don't want to stand in the way of your happiness with someone else. If you want Rick, you should explore that." He shook his head and wiped the palm of his hand over his face in an aggravated sigh. "But just being near you pushes me over the edge, Emily. I just... I just needed

WILDS OF THE HEART

you to know how I truly felt."

A tidal wave of emotion rushed through me. With every blink, I felt closer to the edge of something, but I didn't know what.

Tears?

Happiness?

Joy?

Fear?

I shook my head, and Lucas's expression fell. My breath hitched when I realized he thought that was my answer.

I had no answer.

He started toward the room with the boxes, but I grabbed his wrist. "No, Lucas. That wasn't it."

Lucas turned toward me, and I could feel his gaze etching into my soul, waiting for me to say something.

"I had no idea," I said softly.

He rubbed the back of his neck and shoulder and let out a gust of air, nodding. "I thought you had some inkling. I've tried asking you out a million times."

"I thought you were kidding. We're complete opposites. I like the country. You like the city. I like staying in. You like being out. I read. You don't."

His lips rolled into a smile, and he laughed.

For a second, I let myself imagine what it would be like to be in a relationship with Lucas.

But I couldn't.

I could only see the end, where my heart got broken because he got bored.

"You get easily bored," I said softly. "What if you get tired of me?"

"I could never get tired of you."

"You don't know that. I'm really annoying. High-maintenance."

"Anyone who has food as old as you do in the kitchen can't be that high-maintenance," he teased, and I let out the breath I'd been holding in.

That right there was what was so special between us. We could tease one another and talk about anything and everything.

Except us.

"What if we lose what we have?" I reached out and squeezed his muscular arm, which only drew my thoughts back to the kiss.

Being held in his arms.

"We won't."

"We don't know that."

He took a step toward me and smiled. "We can take it slow."

I lifted my brows. "With a kiss like that, I'm not sure that's possible."

Confidence washed over Lucas's features, and my stomach stirred.

"So, travel…" he said, looping his arms around me, pulling me in. He kissed the top of my head. "I think that's something we have in common."

I loved feeling his lips skate across my head. I'd always liked it when he did that. I didn't know why. Maybe on some level, it felt like he was protecting me, but this time, it felt different.

A good different.

"Well, I won't be traveling anywhere for at least six weeks. Grandparent duty. But I've got my books."

Lucas nodded. "Let me help you with Mimi."

I laughed, shaking my head. "You do not want that stress. Mimi is a handful. If this had been my other grandma, sure. But Mimi will make you run screaming with your tail between your legs."

"Nah. She likes me." Lucas stood tall, and I couldn't help but love him a little more.

That was the problem with starting a relationship with my best friend. There was already love there. I just wasn't sure it was the right kind. I knew lust was heavily pressing into every cell in my body, but with Lucas, I needed to be alert.

Guarded.

Just in case.

I let out a deep breath, and Lucas's gaze fastened on mine. "What are you thinking?"

"That this wasn't what I expected when you came over." I walked into the spare room, sliding my fingers against my lips. The tingle from his mouth over mine was still raw, and it was hard not to ask for more.

He followed behind me. "What did you expect?"

"I thought you were going to tell me that you were interested in Clara. That things needed to cool down between us in the friendship department."

He flinched at the sound of her name. His eyes

got huge. "I told you I have zero feelings for her. Zero."

I nodded, feeling guilty for bringing her up again. "I know you said that, but…"

"But what?"

"There was obviously something there at some point."

Apprehension filled his gaze as his chin tipped up. "I don't think puppy love exactly counts as something being there, other than teenage hormones."

I shrugged, thinking about my sister Mae and her secret crush from high school. All these years, and she still couldn't shake him. "That can lead to something, sometimes."

"True, but it's not the case in this instance." He softly touched my chin and lifted it as my eyes met his. "There was a betrayal there that… let's just say that I'm not sure a person can outgrow it."

"Did she cheat on you?"

"It's more complicated than that."

Which led me to another thought. It was more of a friend question.

"Have you ever cheated on a girlfriend?"

Lucas shook his head. "Never."

I believed him, partially because I doubted he'd held a relationship down long enough to lean into someone else.

His eyes stayed on mine. "You?"

I laughed softly and shook my head, letting out a sigh. "I don't know if you've noticed anything about my dating life in this past year of being friends, but I'm not exactly going out a lot. There's not an opportunity to have a relationship, let alone a moment for me to drop my hook into the fishing pond."

"See? It's not so hard moving past friendship. We can still talk about things like before," he said, grabbing another box. "But now, we can kiss."

He balanced a box on his knee and swept his mouth along my cheek.

"Is that the only difference?" I asked, still wondering about Clara.

Something had obviously bitten him badly for him to talk about her that way. There had never been a hint of betrayal or heartbreak mentioned in his dating life until she popped up out of the blue.

"One thing, Lucas."

He'd made his way into the hallway. "What's that?" His voice was muffled as he climbed the steps to the attic.

"I don't think we should sleep with each other until we're absolutely certain our relationship isn't interfering with our friendship, or vice versa. And I don't want anyone to know that we might start seeing each other."

"Whatever you say, babe," he said from the attic, but I suddenly felt like there was no turning back and I might have made the biggest mistake.

Chapter Ten

Lucas

I rang the doorbell at Emily's bungalow and let out a deep breath. It had been a week since I'd seen her, and I wanted to drop off some coffee and pastries from Mae's new coffee shop.

It was like the moment Emily and I admitted maybe there was something more there, she froze up.

Had I not memorized every detail of the kiss we'd shared, I'd almost think we didn't experience it.

Or the grownup version was that her grandparents had just moved in with her, and she had very little time.

But I'd noticed the texts had dwindled, and when I'd popped in over at the antique store, I'd barely gotten a hello, which would have concerned me, but there were a lot of customers.

So, I thought this might be the best way to lighten her burden and get to say hi.

When she swung open the front door, she looked even more breathtaking than last time I saw her. Her bright green eyes gleamed with a wild expression, her makeup-less face looked fresh, and her dark hair had been twisted into a wet knot anchored on top of her head with a clip.

Her eyes landed on the tray of lattes. "I did not expect you, but thank you."

"You doing okay?" I asked, noticing her avoiding my gaze.

"Just swamped." She lowered her voice. "Mimi is a handful. Do you realize that even when I'm at the store, I get like a few texts an hour from her? And it's not like Grandpa isn't here with her."

She glanced over her shoulder before pulling me inside. "She doesn't like my choice in breakfast cereal, hates plain bagels, only likes cream cheese with chives, and refuses to drink regular coffee. And that's just breakfast."

"Hey, if she's getting cereal that hasn't glued itself together, I'd call that a win out of your pantry."

She giggled, and I detected the lightness I'd grown so accustomed to with Emily.

"You don't need to do this by yourself. I wasn't kidding when I said to call me for help," I offered.

She shook her head and took the tray of drinks from me. "Mimi doesn't even want my other sisters stopping by. Something about not wanting everyone to remember her like this. Whatever that means."

"It's her pride," her grandpa said, quietly walking into the kitchen. He smiled at Emily and nodded. "She trusts you. Knows you'd never hold anything over her head."

"My sisters wouldn't do that either," Emily said softly.

"No. I know they wouldn't, but Mimi has always felt closest to you. I think she sees herself in you the most."

Emily looked surprised, handing her grandpa a latte while I walked over to a cabinet and grabbed some plates for the pastries.

"I never would have guessed that." Emily shook her head.

"You're her little wildflower. Your mom was right about that description of you, and Mimi picked up on it."

Emily touched the pendant on her necklace. "How so?"

"Wildflowers are resilient, persistent, and patiently wait until the conditions are just right." Her grandfather winked at her. "And they like to spread their beauty with the wind to share joy with others while experiencing new growing conditions for themselves. She likes to think of you as always following your heart, never being afraid of doing something on a whim."

Emily smiled, nodding. "I don't know about the spreading with the wind bit, Grandpa. I'm pretty happy with Curiosity Bay."

"What do you think all that reading is about? You don't have to physically be somewhere to experience something new. Your mind is being opened to new conditions of the human spirit by the very words you read."

Her grandpa looked at me and smiled. "Fancy seeing you here this morning."

"Just thought I could drop off some breakfast and coffee." I glanced around the kitchen, hoping he'd pick up on the assortment I'd brought from Mae's coffee shop.

Her grandpa winked at me. "Is that what you kids call it these days?"

"Grandpa, he didn't stay the night. We're just friends," she assured him.

Hearing those words was like a dagger to my heart, mainly because I felt she still believed it.

Her grandpa looked at me, and I realized that I couldn't hide my feelings for Emily. Not any longer. Everyone who looked at me could probably see them stamped on my forehead.

I was falling in love with her, even if she didn't see it.

Even if she was going to be off somewhere for three months writing poetry.

Emily put a pastry on each plate and looked over at me, hoping I would play along with her version of our relationship.

And I had promised that we wouldn't say anything until we knew that we wouldn't ruin our friendship by taking that next step.

But it felt like Emily had sidelined the whole idea. I wasn't so sure she had any plans to be more than just friends with me. If anything, that kiss had derailed any prospect of something more.

If the lack of texts was an indication, I was in trouble, and the idea of dating Emily wasn't even in the cards.

But that kiss...

I'd never felt something so much in my soul as when I held Emily in my arms. The way she folded into me and let go as our kisses deepened...

I knew neither of us wanted the kiss to end. That wasn't something that could be made up.

The chemistry was there, so why did she pull back?

It couldn't just be because we're friends, right?

"Yup. Just friends." I nodded, handing her grandpa a plate with a pecan roll on it.

"We really appreciate everything you're doing for us," her grandpa said to Emily.

"It's nothing," Emily assured him, reaching for his arm and giving it a little squeeze.

"It very much is something." He smiled and took a bite of the pecan roll. "Mmm. Your sister is onto something. I predict great things for that coffee shop."

"Me too." I took a bite of the croissant and sipped on my latte.

A clunking sound rattled down the hall toward the kitchen, and Emily spun around. I followed her gaze to see Mimi in a vibrant purple flannel nightgown. Two tennis balls scuffed along the floor as she pushed and wheeled herself into the kitchen.

"Good morning, Lucas," she said with a gleam in her eyes.

"Good morning, Mimi." I smiled as her eyes stayed on mine.

Emily looked at me perturbed since Mimi forgot to say hello to her.

The family dynamic between these three made me chuckle.

"It sounded like a party in here, and you know how I love a good party." She glanced at the pastries. "A savior. I'm so tired of dried-out bagels."

Mimi patted my shoulder and started to roll away. "Good man. Good man."

She walked right past Emily and made her way into the small dining room while I tried to hold in a laugh.

Emily eyed me.

"She only takes breakfast in the formal dining room. Apparently, it's what her butler does at home," Emily joked.

"Ah, I see," I whispered, reaching for the plate with a cinnamon bun. "Hopefully, she'll be okay with this type of pastry since the others all have bites in them."

Emily chuckled and let out a breath of satisfaction. "Cinnamon anything is her favorite. I learned that yesterday when I defrosted some pumpkin loaf out of my freezer instead of the cinnamon raisin bread. I heard about it via texts up until around three o'clock."

I snickered and shook my head as her grandpa followed Mimi into the other room. "Why don't you let me drive you to work today, and I'll pick you up with some pizza for everyone tonight?"

Emily grimaced and shook her head. "I don't know how Mimi will feel about pizza. She doesn't usually like dinners that you have to pick up and hold."

"Something tells me if I'm the one delivering it, pizza will be just fine, and I'll give her a fork and knife." I didn't wait for Emily's reply and wandered into the dining room with the latte and pastry as Mimi got settled at the end of the dining table with pillows propped behind her.

Maybe I needed to get Emily's family on board with the idea of *us* before Emily would truly warm up to the idea.

At this point, I'd try anything.

Mimi clapped her hands and nodded. "Cinnamon buns. My absolute favorite. Lucas, you're a doll. I only wish Emily would get it through her thick skull what a great guy you are."

I laughed, sliding the cup and plate in front of her. "Me too."

Emily walked in with both hands flying to her

hips. "Hey, now. I know what a great guy Lucas is. He's sweet, charming, and good-looking."

Mimi didn't look amused with her granddaughter's assessment. "So, what's the problem, then?"

I chuckled and cocked my head, waiting for Emily's response.

"He's slowly wearing me down," she confessed. "But we make great friends."

"You might make better lovers." Mimi grinned, and I swore I saw Emily leap back about ten feet.

Her grandpa elbowed me and laughed. "Sometimes, that's gotta be the way with these gals. Just put it all out there."

Mimi took a bite of the pastry and closed her eyes. "Are these from Mae's?"

I nodded.

"She's so talented. I'm glad she decided to break away from the antique store." She looked at Emily. "Is that something you ever think about doing?"

Emily scowled. "Quit Baubles and Curiosities?"

Mimi waited for a reply.

"No, I love it there." She smiled at me. "In fact, I need to get going, or I'll be late."

"Oh, and I'm bringing pizza back tonight for everyone," I told Mimi and her grandpa.

"That sounds wonderful, dear. Thank you for thinking of us." Mimi smiled happily at me, and I could tell Emily wanted to shove me out the door.

Mission Accomplished.

I walked into the kitchen and polished off my croissant as Emily went to her bedroom. I took a couple of sips from the latte and heard her grandparents talking in the other room.

Making my way down the hall, it was hard not to have all the emotions from last week consume me. Thinking back to Emily's hair tangled between my fingers, her mouth pressed against mine, the sweet taste of her lips.

It didn't matter that her grandparents were in the other room. That's what she did to me.

I tapped lightly on her bedroom door.

"Come in," she said softly. "I'm just putting on some mascara."

I walked into her bedroom and stood, glancing around. It seemed as fresh and sweet as Emily with the bright white duvet cover, wildflower pillows, and a few photos on her dresser. I noticed one of her and me and couldn't stop the smile from spreading across my expression.

"You mad at me for buttering up Mimi?" I teased, walking into the bathroom where she was standing.

She laughed and dipped the wand of mascara into the tube. "It makes me question Mimi's BS radar."

"Hey, I wasn't BSing anyone," I said softly. "I'm genuinely picking up pizza."

Her gaze connected with mine in the mirror, and she smiled. "Thanks for not telling them about... us."

I leaned against the doorframe and nodded. "What's there to tell? We're just friends, right?"

She focused on her lashes and nodded. "Exactly."

"But I hope we can be more, maybe when you get back from the residency."

She let out a groan and shook her head, taking a step forward. "I just don't think you're seeing things clearly right now. And we don't know that I'm headed anywhere, remember?"

Emily rested her hands on my chest and looked into my eyes.

"You only want me because you can't have me. Or worse yet, because Rick did. What happens when you get me?"

If only she knew the power of her own words.

Chapter Eleven

Emily

It slipped out, but it had to be said. Why else would Lucas Edwards be so infatuated with me? He could get any woman he wanted. That much was clear, and he didn't seem to want any of them at the moment. But when I made it my mission not to want him, he became interested.

Reverse psychology at its best.

And that worried me.

And it couldn't be overlooked that none of this came up until he saw Rick and me exchanging numbers.

I stared at my brother standing by a stack of comic books he'd picked up on his latest flea market road trip.

He'd probably be the best person to talk about all

this with. After all, Brad and Lucas were probably more alike than they knew.

"What's up, my little M&M?" Brad grinned, leaning against the glass case. "I saw Lucas dropped you off. How's that going?"

"How's what going?"

His brows curled into exasperation. "We all see how he looks at you."

I folded my arms over my chest. "Yeah? And how's that?"

He propped himself off the counter and shrugged. "Just thought there might be something there, that's all."

"Just friends," I assured him.

My brother studied me closely and didn't say anything for a few seconds. "Are you sure about that?"

"Yeah, I'm pretty certain I'd know if we were more than friends." My cheeks warmed as I shoved the memories of the kiss out of my head.

My brother chuckled, wiping his thumb back and forth against the stubble on his jawline. "Whatever you say."

"What about you?" I asked. "Do you ever see yourself settling down?"

He shrugged. "Yeah. Why not? If I find the right girl, I could see it."

"But how will you know you've found the right one?"

"I imagine that I'll just know." He nodded. "There'll be something *different* about us."

I nodded and let out a sigh. "But until then?"

"I guess I'll just continue to have fun."

I grinned, glancing at my brother. He looked like the rest of us, with dark hair and green eyes, but he took after my dad when it came to temperament. He was boisterous, outgoing, and super flirty. My mom had passed down a more mystical disposition where we believed in something less obvious, some more romantic notion to guide us.

Even when it came to running the store, we all felt attachments to certain objects that would come into the store. Some of us could sense things from the prior owners or the object's history or imagine where the object should settle in its next stage. But not Brad. He'd just go sort through stacks of comic books and dive into boxes of toy trucks and be done with it.

Of all the sisters, I'd say Audrey might have those tendencies as well. She was more of a face-value kind of gal. I sometimes envied them. It seemed simpler to just put yourself out there and not worry about the implications.

"By fun, you mean an assortment?" I teased my brother.

Brad eyed me curiously. "Are you catching feelings for someone? Is it Lucas? You never ask me about my dating life."

"Love isn't a virus," I said, laughing. "I'm not catching anything, and especially not for Lucas. I know better. I think he's only starting to raise a brow in my direction because he saw Rick and me exchanging numbers."

"Rick, huh?" Brad chewed on his bottom lip. "Interesting."

"No, it wasn't like that. Rick just offered to help because of Mimi and Grandpa."

My brother chuckled. "No, of course not. Men

always love to drop everything they're doing to help out with the elderly."

I frowned, thinking about what he said. It wasn't like that. Was it?

"You could have a line of men circling the store for you, and I doubt you'd notice," he added.

I laughed, glancing around the store. "Yet, that's not happening, is it?"

Not to mention, if they were lining up, it was clearly for date one.

Brad smiled, shaking his head. "I wish you saw what I saw in you, Em."

"Well, there's nothing between Rick and me." I swallowed down the words on the tip of my tongue about Lucas.

"And Lucas?"

Darn it.

"I don't know. He's cute and kind. Who knows?"

"I'm not sure I like him for one of my sisters." Brad shook his head. "It's smart to be cautious."

Amelia walked over and set a plate on the glass counter. "Cautious about what?"

"Lucas," Brad filled her in. "I told her I don't trust him."

Amelia scrunched her face. "Why not? He's a sweetheart."

Brad laughed and shook his head. "A sweetheart? Where'd you come up with that? That guy's socials are blowing up with DMs. Mark. My. Words."

The thought made my stomach roil with tension. "How do you know that?"

"Have you ever scrolled through his profiles?" Brad smirked, stretching toward the ceiling.

I laughed and shook my head. "No, have you?"

Brad reached for his phone out of his back pocket. "No, but I can tell just by looking at the guy that he's popular with the ladies."

Amelia cocked her head to the side. "You are so weird."

"I call it as I see it." Brad smiled.

"Maybe you and Lucas are just two peas in a pod," I said, trying to act like I wasn't all that interested. "It doesn't matter, anyway. We're just friends."

"Just friends?" Amelia stared at me.

Had Lucas told his cousin that we'd kissed?

"Yeah. Just friends. Why?"

"You guys are just cute together." Amelia patted my back.

Brad rolled his eyes. "They're not cute together. That guy is not getting a piece of my sister."

"Excuse me?" I asked. "Since when do you have a say in whom I'm interested in?"

"See? I knew you were interested in him." Brad laughed and shook his head. "I just wanted to see if I could get a rise out of you. Besides, it's clear as day that you like Lucas. It's only a matter of time, even if I don't like the guy."

"That's not true, but you don't even know him," I pointed out.

"I don't have to know him." He pushed the phone in front of me. "Look at all the likes on his photos. They're all females."

"That doesn't prove anything," I said, dismissing my brother's accusations, but I couldn't help but eye a few of the posts. "That doesn't mean he's busy messaging them, and besides, we aren't together, so it doesn't matter if he was busy messaging them."

Dottie wandered over and snorted as if she disagreed with my brother too.

I noticed his latest showed he was on the island. Maybe I should scan his posts more often.

And then my eye caught a recent like by someone named Clara Honler.

I pulled my brother's phone close and brought up her profile.

Yup, that was the same Clara.

I tried to push away the annoying feelings pummeling through my veins.

What was it about that single like? Some sort of vague jealousy? I had no right to be jealous, and it wasn't like he'd liked something of hers. It had been the other way around.

But it did prove he was on her radar. I stared at the photo and saw the date. It was a photo of him at the beach on the morning of our trip to see the mystery writer. He was at our spot. I had no idea he'd been there that morning. I just assumed he was working until we left for Seattle.

I let out a deep breath and thought about that day. He'd gone to so much trouble to surprise me. Were things changing between us whether I wanted them to or not?

Shoving the phone back to my brother, I stood up and let out a sigh as I brought my eyes to his.

"See what I mean?"

I nodded. "I don't think he's busy texting all those women back. He shouldn't be penalized for being good-looking."

"Emily, you're gorgeous. Do you get a hundred men hitting like on each photo?"

I scowled at my brother. "Actually, I do."

Not true.

All my accounts were private.

Amelia chuckled. "Okay, you two. Break it up. I'm headed upstairs to do inventory on all our broaches."

When my sister was out of range, I leaned over the cabinet. "Do you think you'd know if you met the girl of your dreams right away or…" I looked up at my brother. "Or would it take a few times before you knew she was the one?"

He smiled. "I'd like to think I'll see her, and I'll know."

"That would be nice, wouldn't it?"

"Here's hoping." He put a stack of comics on a shelf. "Hey, I'm scheduled to hit a few garage sales and flea markets next week, but the vet just told me she couldn't watch Oscar."

A chill settled over me, and I frantically shook my head. "No. Absolutely not, Brad. I'm not watching Oscar. He's mean. No, he's more than mean. He wants blood."

"Oscar's not that bad. He's just misunderstood. I can't put him in boarding," Brad pleaded.

"Even the vet is scared of him, Brad." I shook my head. "Until you get him a meeting with a priest, I don't want anything to do with him. He'll eat me when I'm sleeping."

"He would not. He'd wait until you're awake." Brad laughed. "He'd enjoy it more."

I laughed. "Exactly. But did you forget I'm already taking care of Mimi and Grandpa? My plate is full. Go ask someone else to be your mercenary."

Brad smiled and nodded. "I'll find someone."

"I'm sure you will."

The bell dinged for our door, and I spun around.

It was like the air had been knocked right out of me.

She walked in with her head held up high as she scanned the store. Sunglasses sat propped on her head as her messy blonde hair bounced with each step. She wore a tight pair of jeans and an even tighter red top. A boy in his late teens walked in behind her. He looked like he'd rather be anywhere other than an antique store on some small island.

I glanced at my brother, who looked intrigued, and rolled my eyes at him.

What was Clara doing here?

"You want to go help the customer?" I asked.

"If you insist," he said, grinning.

But it was too late. She spotted me and wandered over with a big smile.

"What a small world," she said. "Aren't you friends with Lucas?"

I nodded slowly, trying to figure out how in the

world she'd managed to show up here, of all places.

"Wow. Good to see you. Clara, right?" I asked, and she grinned wider.

I wish I could say it felt genuine.

"This is my son," she told me, pointing at him to come over.

He pushed his mouth into a forced smile and nodded. "Nice to meet you." It was barely above a mumble but not too bad for a teenager.

My brother walked over. "You two know one another?"

"Through a mutual friend," she said.

The tension in my stomach knotted into a million little achy kinks.

"Oh, yeah? Who's that?"

"Lucas Edwards," Clara relayed.

My brother's brows knitted together. "Oh, I see."

"I used to date him. A long time ago." She waved her hands around.

"You don't say." Brad nodded and glanced at her son, who'd wandered toward the comic book section.

I knew exactly what my brother was thinking.

This was proof that Lucas wasn't good boyfriend material. He had random women showing up in not-so-random places.

But I knew how Lucas felt about Clara.

Didn't I?

"What brings you to Marigold?" Brad asked.

She laughed. "Actually, I saw a lot of tags for this location from Luke, and I wanted to see where he'd been spending so much time." Her eyes focused on me. "And now I know why."

Luke? No one really called him Luke except maybe little Henry.

"That's not creepy at all," Brad whispered as she walked over to her son.

I looked at my brother. "I'm so confused."

My brother's eyes widened as he watched Clara and her son wandering the store. "Do you think Lucas knows she's here?"

"Uh, no." I cleared my throat. "But I could be wrong."

"You should text him." Brad's brows waggled up and down.

I elbowed my brother and chuckled. "You're such a pot stirrer. But you know what?"

"Tell me."

"None of this bothers me."

"No, of course not."

I glanced at Clara. "Do you know why?"

"I can only imagine."

"Because we're just friends."

"Right." Brad nodded. "Just friends."

Clara bent down and picked up the pink poodle I'd put out a few weeks ago, and my brows knitted together in concern.

"That's not the right home for that."

Brad looked around. "For what?"

"The pink poodle."

"Money is money," Brad muttered.

"Not like this." I shook my head as she took it to the counter.

I walked over and smiled at Clara. "I'm sorry. That's not for sale."

She looked puzzled. "It's on the floor with a price."

"Sorry." I shook my head. "It's just a mistake."

"But it would be perfect for my family's white elephant party."

I gasped at the thought of the poodle becoming a joke. "Someone else already bought it. Sorry."

Clara tilted her chin and glanced at her son. "Okaay."

"Sorry about that."

"That's fine." She shrugged, touching a necklace my sister had just put out this morning. I wanted to grab it away from her too, but I held back.

And then I realized it.

The bits of jealousy nipping at me were only going to get worse until I confronted the truth about what Lucas meant to me.

Chapter Twelve

Lucas

I'd ordered the pizza and was just picking up some tea and dessert at the grocery store when I looked up and saw Emily's brother.

He looked over at me but didn't smile.

Seemed about right.

"Hey there, Brad." I lifted my basket. "Just grabbing some stuff for Mimi and everyone."

Brad looked surprised. "Yeah?"

The incessant beeping from the self-checkout peppered the awkward silence as Brad made his way over.

I nodded. "I'm picking up a pizza over at Pete's and then picking up Emily."

"Really," Brad said flatly. "You sure you got

your names right? You know, man to man."

"I have no idea what you're talking about, but yeah… I'm picking up Emily when she gets off work."

"Not Clara?" His eyes drilled into me.

My chest tightened. What did he know about Clara?

I straightened my shoulders and rested the basket on a fruit stand. "Not Clara. No."

What had Emily said to her brother? Was that the issue with this whole taking it to the next level thing? Clara?

"She showed up at the store today." Brad stared at me.

"Clara?" I blurted out. "Why would she do that?"

"I was hoping you had the answer for that."

I let out a deep breath and shook my head. "Man, I have no idea."

"Are you leading my sister on?" He folded his arms over his chest.

"I wish I could, Brad." I stared right back.

"Then what's up with this other woman?"

"She's a girlfriend from high school who just got

a divorce and moved back to the city. How do I know all this? I wanted to surprise Emily with tickets to see her favorite author, but Clara's best friend was the PR woman in charge of doling out sold-out tickets. I had no idea they were still in contact, but when Emily and I arrived, we both got an earful."

He slapped my shoulder. "Well, buddy. It looks like you got yourself a stalker if you're telling me you haven't led her on."

"The only thing I told her was that I wasn't interested. That's it. Why she's here is beyond me."

"I hope that's true."

"Actions speak louder than words." I scanned the aisles, suddenly paranoid that Clara was going to jump out of nowhere. "I haven't reached out to her, and I have no interest in doing so."

"I see."

"Anyway, you're more than welcome to join us for dinner."

Brad shook his head. "No, I gotta go home. Oscar hasn't seen me in a while, and he missed me."

"Oscar? Your cat?"

He nodded. "Hey, come to think of it…"

"What's up?"

"I'm headed back out for a quick road trip next week, and everywhere is booked. You think you could watch him?"

I'd heard about this cat.

But seriously. How crazy could a cat be?

Maybe I'd score some points, and by the looks of it, I needed any help I could get with her brother.

"Sure. Yeah. I can stay at the orchard and bring him there."

"Awesome. Thanks, man. I'll be in touch when it gets closer." He started toward the produce section.

"Hey, Brad…"

He glanced at me. "Yeah?"

"Has Emily mentioned anything about me?"

"Not much." He shook his head. "No, but I'm sure having your ex show up at the store isn't a great way to prove that you're boyfriend material." Brad laughed. "I'm no expert, but my gut says that's not good."

"I'll keep that in mind. Thanks." I walked to the self-checkout and started scanning my items as I thought about Clara showing up on the island. I hoped Brad was only kidding about Clara's intentions, but he seemed to know more about things than I certainly did.

As I made my way out the door with my groceries, I walked over to my car and heard the shrill sound of Clara's voice ringing in my ears.

I popped open my trunk and put the groceries down, pretending I didn't hear her.

That only made her louder.

Shutting the trunk, I took a deep breath and let it out slowly as she called my name again and wove through the parked cars.

"Luke," she called.

My jaw tensed. The only person who called me Luke was Henry. She'd ruined that name for me a long time ago.

I slowly turned to see Clara sliding along two cars to get to me, and I swallowed down the annoyance.

Great.

Just what I needed with Brad inside.

"I wondered if I'd bump into you," Clara said, now only a couple of feet away.

"What are you doing here?" My voice sounded gruff, but she was lucky it wasn't worse.

"Just wanted to show my son around, and I saw a lot of the pictures you've posted of Marigold Island. It looked beautiful."

Okay. Maybe Brad was overreacting.

"And maybe on some level, I hoped I'd bump into you."

I shook my head. "Why would you think that?"

"You had your location turned on, and you posted a pic this morning outside some coffee shop."

I looked at the boy standing behind her. It was hard not to be taken aback.

"So you took a ferry ride this morning because I was here?"

She laughed, touching her chest. "When you put it that way, it sounds a little crazy."

"Well, I'm sorry to be rude, but I have someone to pick up."

"Is it your friend at the antique store?" she asked as I opened the door to my car.

"That's really not your business, Clara." I

glanced at her son, not wanting to humiliate his mom in front of him. "But it's good to see you again. Have a nice evening."

I sat in my seat, shut the door, and turned on the car.

I glanced up to see Brad coming out of the store with a bag of groceries, and his gaze landed on Clara immediately before turning his attention to me as I pulled out of the stall.

By the time I pulled up to Baubles and Curiosities, I was totally amped up and completely worried about what she'd done or said to Emily when she'd stopped by.

And I was madder at myself for not turning off location services, but who would actually try to follow me?

The whole thing just boggled my mind.

I glanced up at the entrance of Baubles and Curiosities to see the door open and Rick step outside. His smile was as wide as the Cheshire Cat's as he stepped onto the sidewalk with Emily. She looked into his eyes and laughed.

Fear arose deep and raw when I looked at her with another man.

Would she be happier with someone else?

It looked easy between those two.

But with me?

I shook my head.

My past was catching up with me in more ways than one, and all I wanted was for the one girl I'd fallen helplessly in love with to fall too.

The things we'd shared with one another and felt weren't…

It wasn't in my head.

We had something special.

I did a light tap on my horn despite my best efforts to contain myself. I wasn't a jealous person, but this was agonizing.

She looked over and smiled with a quick wave as Rick nodded and made his way down the sidewalk.

Emily wandered over, carrying a pink porcelain poodle with her, and I couldn't help but laugh when she opened the door.

"What the heck is that thing? Didn't you just put

it out on the floor awhile back?"

"Funny you should ask." She slid into the front seat and shut the door.

"Your girlfriend—"

"I don't have a girlfriend," I interrupted. "You made that clear."

"Fine. Your ex-girlfriend tried to buy it, and she doesn't deserve it. So, I'm putting it in my bedroom until she gets off the island."

"I see." I pulled onto the main road and snuck a look at Emily.

So, she was bothered by Clara's sudden appearance. I tapped the wheel to the music playing as we drove through town to the pizza place.

Maybe she did have feelings for me.

"Rick just hanging out?" I asked.

She turned to me and eyed me carefully. "Would it matter?"

I shrugged.

"Why do you have so many women following you on social media?" I could feel her frown on me.

"What are you talking about?"

"My brother pointed out that most of your interaction is with females, and he said your DMs are probably blowing up too."

I chuckled, shaking my head. "Did he, now…"

"He did, and he was right. I'd just never paid attention before."

"Well, news flash." I glanced at her as I pulled into the parking lot. "I've never paid attention either."

"Hmph." She brought the pink porcelain poodle closer.

I shut off the car and turned to look at Emily. "But we're just friends, right? That's why you've stopped texting me back much. It's why we haven't hung out much since the kiss."

She sat silently and dropped her gaze to the poodle.

"You regret it, don't you?"

Emily didn't respond.

"You're keeping me at a distance, and you didn't want to tell me."

She brought her gaze to mine. She was so pretty.

"It's not like that." She let out a slow breath.

"I've just been really busy with my grandparents."

I nodded and drew a breath. "Okay. If that's your story. I'll go grab the pizza."

She smiled at me, but it felt different.

Maybe the kiss wasn't as mind-blowing for her as it had been for me.

Damn, these thoughts.

I'd never been so confused in my life over a woman.

Then again, I'd never felt this way for someone before.

Ever.

I walked up to the entrance of Pete's Pizza and opened the door. The immediate smells of sweet tomato sauce and spicy garlic drifted over as I made my way to the counter to pick up the two pizzas and a batch of garlic knots.

Nothing said friendship like a meal of pure garlic.

"Hey, Lucas," Pete said, smiling. "Long time, no see."

"It's been too long." I nodded in agreement. "But I'm hoping to change that."

"Oh, yeah?"

"I hope to spend more of the spring and summer here for sure. In fact, I'll be here next week because I'm watching Brad's cat."

Pete flinched and hissed. "Have you gone mad? Everyone knows to stay away from that beast."

I chuckled, reaching for the boxes.

"Just trying to impress a girl, Pete."

His brows moved up. "One of the Evans girls."

I laughed, nodding as I walked toward the exit. "Afraid so."

"Good luck," he called and then muttered, "You'll need it."

As I pushed my way out the door, I couldn't help but notice the lavender sky with hot pink streaks as vivid as any wildflower out there.

I put the pizzas in the back and smiled when I spotted what Emily was looking at. She tried to hide her phone under the poodle, but it was too late.

"Find anything interesting?" I asked.

She stared out the window. "I don't know what you're talking about."

"Did you like my photos?"

She grunted and turned to face me. "Fine. Yes. You post good pictures."

A rumble of a laugh escaped my lips, which only made her flash a dirty look in my direction.

As I pulled out of the parking lot, I could feel Emily's eyes on me. I looked over, and she looked away.

"Okay. What's going on between us?" I asked.

"We kissed, Lucas." She sighed. "And that changed everything."

"How could it have changed everything?" I asked, feeling the tension rise in my chest.

Just like I'd worried. Something wasn't right.

"We shared one kiss. You made me promise not to tell a soul." I cleared my throat. "And we can't sleep together, so... tell me how anything has changed."

"They just have," she said softly. The tenderness in her voice worried me. It felt like a tidal wave of emotions was going to slam down on me at any moment.

After a minute or two of silence, she adjusted herself in the seat and looked at me.

"It's just not a good idea to date."

And in an instant, my entire world imploded. I could see it in her eyes. Our friendship had already changed. She'd made sure that happened the moment our kiss ended.

Chapter Thirteen

Emily

It stung that Lucas didn't even hang around for the pizza. He'd just walked it up to the house, placed it on the kitchen table, and turned around and left.

There wasn't any playful banter, no hugs, and no text you laters.

That kiss had thoroughly screwed things up, just as I'd worried it would.

I finally had a day off from the store, and Mimi was doing much better. I'd gone grocery shopping for a couple of items like butter and bread and decided to stop by the beach. It was the same place Lucas and I would go sometimes.

There weren't all that many areas around the island that had public access to a flat area of beach. This little place was like an oasis.

Seagulls swooped around overhead as I traversed the rocky beach until I could make it over to the boulder.

It had been a week since I'd seen Lucas, and the distance had hurt. I missed having my friend. There hadn't been a day gone by where one of us didn't send some sort of funny meme or joke. Text something goofy one of us did, or just say a simple *hi*.

But since the kiss, it had all stopped. It was partly my fault. I didn't know what to say or how to be flirty with Lucas.

So, I'd just stared at my blank screen and decided to write nothing.

Another thing that changed was my genre preference. I couldn't crack a mystery to save my life.

I craved poems. I needed the solitude of very few words to convey some sort of meaning.

But I was also tired. It was exhausting taking care of Mimi and Grandpa. Granted, they'd settled in, and Mimi had stopped complaining about my food selection as much, partly because I got everything on her grocery list, but just worrying about her safety in my house wore me out.

I closed my eyes and listened to the gentle lapping of waves against the pebble beach.

Things would be okay.

As Grandma Cecilia always said, *This too shall pass.*

I missed Lucas, but it would all sort itself out.

It had to.

"Hey, Emily." I heard Lucas's voice and blinked my eyes open to see him walking along the shoreline in a pair of jeans that hugged his thick thighs, a blue thermal with the sleeves pushed up, and some hiking boots. He looked sensational, as usual. I ripped my gaze away and looked out toward the water.

"I didn't expect you to be here," I said, not looking over at him.

"I was on the way to the orchard and saw your scooter parked up top." He traversed the rocky beach in my direction and smiled. "Hope you don't mind the company."

I shook my head. "Not at all."

And it was true.

"I was just thinking about us," I confessed.

"Did you come up with anything?" he asked, weaving his fingers together.

"I wish the kiss had never happened."

I saw hurt flicker behind his gaze. "I didn't expect it to damage our friendship." He shook his head and kicked his feet out in front of him. "Or I never would have done it."

"I tried to make it seem normal, but all I can think about is that kiss and what it meant."

He turned to face me. "What did it mean?"

"To me?" I let out a sigh. "It meant that I could lose the one guy in my life who means the world to me."

He didn't say anything. Instead, he reached his arm over and draped it along my shoulders.

"Then let's forget it ever happened. I can do that. We can just pick up where we left off."

I let his words sink in as I slowly nodded in silent agreement.

"But I do feel like it was a bit of a self-fulfilling prophecy. Things didn't have to get weird," he added.

All sorts of emotions swelled up inside me. I

wanted to turn and yell at him for being such a perfect friend, for not pushing me, not fighting for me.

And that was when it hit me.

"I don't want to be like those other girls you date." I shrugged. "I'm the one you call, not them. But once we start dating, that could go away."

He laughed a low rumble of a noise and stared straight ahead. "Don't you get it, Emily? There's nobody like you. You're incredible and special, smart pretty, funny... but most of all, you understand me." He drew a deep breath and nodded. "And I'm pretty sure I understand you more than you realize."

I stared across the beach filled with pebbles of every size, shape, and color. But they all had one thing in common.

They'd been worn down with time.

Maybe that was Lucas's approach too.

I noticed scratches on Lucas's hands and sucked in a breath of worry. "What happened?"

Lucas looked down at his hands and chuckled. "Ah, Oscar. Oscar happened."

My eyes moved up to meet his, and I laughed in

disbelief. "My brother conned you into watching his demonic cat?"

Lucas turned and stretched out against the boulder, propping his elbow on the rock.

"I essentially volunteered."

"Since when do you talk to my brother?"

"We ran into one another at the grocery store… the night I was picking up the pizza, actually."

She nodded. "I'm sorry you got roped into watching that cat."

He shrugged. "It gave me an excuse to stay on the island this week."

Surprise darted through me. I was surprised Brad hadn't mentioned anything.

He really wasn't fond of Lucas.

I couldn't hide my smile, and I shook my head. "I wouldn't wish cat sitting Oscar on my worst enemy, but apparently, Brad would."

Lucas's eyes met mine. "What's that supposed to mean?"

"I'm not sure my brother is that fond of you," I confessed.

"You don't say," Lucas said wryly. "But I don't blame him."

"You don't?"

"Nah. He wants to protect his sister. I'd do the same, except Nina…"

I chuckled, knowing Nina was already a handful. "Yeah, she probably doesn't need protection. No."

"He probably sees himself in me," Lucas added, which surprised me.

"How so?"

"He's a single guy, dating around, not thinking of settling down…" His eyes stayed on mine. "I was like that."

"What changed?"

"I met you," he said simply.

I shook my head and laughed, glancing down the beach to see a couple throwing a stick for their retriever.

"What's so funny?" he teased. "You don't believe me?"

"Your social calendar is as full as ever. If meeting me made you think of settling down, then why did your dating life explode?" My brow arched. "Unless you're telling me you went out even more before you met me."

Lucas scratched his chin, and I noticed the day's stubble shadowing his strong jawline.

He let out a deep breath. "I think I need to confess something to you, Emily."

I shook my head. "Nope. We're just friends. Remember? We're going back to how things were. You don't need to explain a thing to me about your dating life. Maybe you went on three dates a day before you met me. I don't know. I don't need to know."

He chuckled and shook his head. "You're making things pretty difficult."

My hand slid to his knee, and I felt the pull to him again. "Difficult is my middle name."

"It's true, though." A glimmer of hope flickered behind his gaze.

"What's true?"

"That when I met you, things changed."

He moved his hand over mine and squeezed it. "I mean it."

"I appreciate that." I nodded, swallowing down a lump of worry. Would we really be able to get back to what we had? "But actions speak louder than words. If you'd been that into me like you said, don't you think your social calendar would have reflected that?" I straightened and shook my head. "But not my business."

"Maybe things aren't always as they appear." He didn't take his eyes off me. "And it's not like I've been on any dates recently."

I chuckled, pushing down the annoying sensation of jealousy trying to ride into my soul. I'd never been a jealous person, but hearing he hadn't been on a date made me happy.

And it shouldn't matter.

But it did.

He bit his bottom lip and let out a deep breath, and all I wanted to do was lean over and kiss him.

Again.

I squeezed my eyes shut and groaned. "This is going to be so hard."

"What is?"

I opened my eyes and leaned my head against his shoulder. "Not thinking about that kiss, any kiss…"

"So, you're saying that the kiss meant

something."

I laughed. "Obviously."

"It did to me, too." He glanced at me. "Now, to most normal human beings, that would be a sign."

I didn't say anything.

"You know, when two people find each other attractive, have chemistry, and have an amazing friendship, it can lead to something pretty incredible, and a lot of people would jump on that ride to see where it goes."

I chuckled. "But I'm not most people."

"Clearly."

"Tell me about Clara," I said, turning toward him and tucking my leg under me. "She seems a bit... infatuated."

He smiled and laughed, looking uncomfortable. "She's freshly divorced, and I'm just low-hanging fruit."

I chuckled. "Huh?"

He shrugged. "It's true."

"That doesn't really tell me about her, though..." My voice trailed off.

"I don't know much about her now, other than

what you heard from Lydia that day."

I nodded, admiring his dance around divulging what I really wanted to know. I'd try another way.

"So, how many girlfriends did you have back in school?" I asked as a little breeze picked up. I shuddered from the chill, and he wrapped his arm around me.

"I had three," he informed me.

"Three." I nodded.

"How about you?" he asked, still keeping me close.

"One. Senior year. He stole my V-card and broke up with me the next day."

"That's not right." He shook his head. "I'm sorry that happened."

A few minutes of silence sat between us.

"Funny how things from so long ago can screw us up, huh?"

I chuckled and cast him a look. "Who says I'm screwed up?"

He nuzzled my nose quickly and laughed, pulling back. It took everything thing I had not to crawl on top of him and press my lips to his.

"You had three girlfriends," I repeated, nodding. "What would happen if the other two showed up? Same reaction as with Clara?"

He laughed, dropping his arm down. "No. The history was a little different with Clara."

"First   love?"

He smirked and shook his head. "I get where you're going."

"Perfect. Then I don't need to spell it out for you." I smiled wryly at him.

"Clara and I dated for a year and a half. Part of our junior and senior years." He stood and turned to face me. I blocked the sunlight out of my face with my hand and nodded as I focused on his gaze. It didn't leave mine. "She became pregnant."

I froze and immediately thought about Clara's son in my store the other day. He didn't look like Lucas at all, but that happened all the time with kids. They'd take after one parent more than the other.

I didn't know what to say, so I just stayed silent.

"For six months, we kept the secret. I knew my

parents would flip out and not in a good way, and her parents would probably hunt me down." He brushed his fingers along his jaw and let out a low breath. "But the kicker was that I started getting excited instead of being absolutely petrified. It certainly wasn't what I'd planned. The timing was all wrong, but the thought of raising a son actually thrilled me to death."

"I had no idea…" My voice trailed off.

"No. Wait for it." He held up his hand and shook his head.

"What? There's a kicker?"

"So, I started putting together a plan to take care of Clara and the baby. I'd saved up enough for rent because I was fairly certain my parents would not be letting us stay at our house, even though it was a huge place."

"Okay."

"I bought a crib with her, bedding, tiny little onesies… I actually realized how much I wanted this baby, and the whole thing confused me because prior to finding out she was pregnant, I'd planned on ending things with her. She was headed to one college, and I was headed to another. We didn't have anything in common."

I nodded, completely bewildered about where this was going.

He laughed under his breath and took a seat next to me again. "I don't even think she liked me, to be honest. Everything I did annoyed her. I chewed too loudly. She hated my laugh. She thought my clothes were awful." Lucas shrugged and linked his hands together as he leaned over his knees.

"I'd planned a dinner with my parents to let them know I was going to become a father."

"Did James know?"

He shook his head. "He still doesn't. Nobody does."

"Wait. They don't know you have a son?"

Lucas pressed his lips together and looked at me. "I don't have a son. She had lied to me. She slept with my best friend, and he was the father of her child."

My jaw dropped at the news. "I'm... I'm stunned."

Chapter Fourteen

Lucas

A few seconds went by as I watched Emily's reaction. She'd never been great at hiding her feelings, and this moment was no different. Her expression turned from shock, surprise, and confusion to anger.

We were still on the anger stage.

Her gaze flashed to mine, and I saw the fire behind it.

"How dare that woman," she said, shooting up from the boulder. "It's a damn good thing I didn't know that before she tried to buy the poodle, or it would have been cracked over her head."

This was a new side of Emily. I'd never heard her resort to violence. I hid in a chuckle but couldn't believe how much lighter I felt.

It was like carrying around this secret for so many years had been slowly eating away at me, and I didn't even realize it.

"Why didn't you tell anyone?" she asked, coming over to me and sitting back down.

"What would I have said? It was all after the fact." I eyed Emily as her eyes stayed on me. "I'm sure it sounds so weird, but I was actually really disappointed the baby wasn't mine. Had she told me at month two, I doubt I would have given it much thought. But spending all those months preparing made me enthralled with the idea of becoming a dad."

"What did you do with the crib?" Emily asked.

I laughed, shaking my head. "Of all the questions… that's what popped into your head?"

"I'm in retail for a living." She chuckled. "I can't help it."

"I just gave it all to her."

"And your best friend?" she asked softly.

"Let's just say we didn't hang out much after that. I guess I gave her him, too."

"So that is who she married and divorced," she

said matter-of-factly. "Is that why you don't trust women and go through them like they're objects?"

My eyes widened. "I trust women."

Her brows arched into a befuddled expression.

"And I totally respect women. I've never misled anyone or given the impression that I wanted something long-term or…"

She kept her eyes focused on me.

"It would be hard for me to trust women after being lied to like that." She shook her head. "There are so many levels of betrayal with that one scenario that I don't even know what makes me angrier."

"It was rough, but I got over it."

"Until you heard her name." Emily pressed her mouth into a frown and nodded. "All so I could see my favorite author."

I laughed. "Who knew the horrors that would bring?"

Emily smiled and pulled my hand into hers. "Thank you for sharing that with me. I feel… honored." She scowled. "And pissed."

"It was all a long time ago," I said, waving my

hand around. "We were young. People make mistakes."

Emily nodded as her eyes stayed on mine. "But I'd say that's pretty gutsy to try to date you."

"Yeah. There's that." I nodded in agreement. "It kind of told me she hadn't changed much."

"How?"

"I think back in the day, she wasn't really into me. Just the idea of me… and I was like a challenge. Once she became my girlfriend" —I shrugged my shoulders— "I think her mission was over, and she became disinterested."

"My thoughts are still rattling around my brain trying to figure this out." I shook my head. "I just can't imagine leading a guy on, no matter my age, that he's the father of my child when I knew otherwise."

"Well, it takes all kinds."

"We aren't all like that," Emily said softly.

"I know." I tucked a piece of her dark hair back behind her ear and nodded. "I know."

I thought about her words about my not trusting women. Was she onto something? Was that why I never wanted anything serious?

I pushed away the thoughts and focused on my friend in front of me.

Maybe she was right. It was best for us to stay in the friend zone.

Would I have been able to tell her if she were my girlfriend?

"I'm glad I didn't let her buy the poodle," she revealed.

I laughed, pulling her into me, and felt her body relax against mine.

"I missed this," I whispered, the words skating across her hair.

"Me too," she said, looking up at me. "See? This is too important to let slip away."

I nodded, knowing what she meant. But I wanted to believe that there was a way to have the best of both worlds.

Somehow.

Some way.

"Did she ever tell you why she misled you? Was it on purpose or a miscalculation or…?" Emily asked.

I bit my bottom lip and groaned. "I'd like to tell

you it was one of those reasons, but she said she knew from the beginning."

"Okay." Emily waited for me to continue.

She could always tell when there was more to the story.

"She knew I had more money than my friend."

"So, Clara wanted to use you for your money."

"I suppose. Anyway, that is why when I told you there was nothing there and I had zero interest, I meant it. I don't care if she's completely changed. I just... can't."

"No. I get it. It's crystal clear now." She stood from the rock and scanned the water before turning toward me. "I'll let my jealous thoughts drift away." I grinned.

I eyed her, unsure whether she was kidding or not.

"I'd appreciate it if you never told anyone."

Emily pretended to zip her mouth and nodded. "Lips are sealed, but it explains a lot to me. It really does. But I should probably get back home to check on Mimi and Grandpa. I just grabbed a couple of things from the grocery. They'll probably start to worry about me."

I stood and rested my arm over her shoulders as we walked along the rocky beach. The couple had left, and it was just us.

Emily was so understanding.

So gorgeous.

So close.

It was hard not to pull her into my arms and kiss her.

I clenched my jaw and looked away as we walked up the pathway to the parking lot.

When we reached her scooter, she turned and faced me. "Thanks for sharing that with me."

"I wish it changed things between us." I realized I should have kept those words in, but she didn't seem to notice because she darted across the parking lot.

Her hands flailed in the air as she flew across the lot before she bent down and started whispering to the bushes. I quickly followed her lead and knelt down next to her.

"There's a puppy in here," she whispered. "Come here, puppers. Come on."

It was a struggle to focus on the puppy when she was next to me, stretching her arms into the shrubs with her shirt lifting slightly. I pulled my gaze away and strained to see the small dog.

"Come on, buddy," I said, snapping my fingers lightly.

The creature hissed and looked up at us, bearing its pointy teeth and a long, naked tail.

"Emily, that's not a dog." I pulled her into my arms and stood, backing away.

"Of course, it's a dog." She shimmied away from me and bent back down right before she screamed and jumped back again, landing in my arms.

I could feel her heart jumping in her chest as the opossum slinked back into the bushes. She propped her head up and bit her bottom lip as her green eyes stayed on mine.

Kissing her was all I wanted to do in this moment, but I...

Her hands moved to my cheeks, and she lifted herself onto her toes, touching her lips to mine.

My body instantly responded as her soft lips

swept against mine.

Emily's eyes closed as she leaned into me, kissing me some more.

I stood there like stone, feeling every emotion battle inside me until I couldn't resist any longer. Her lips parted as her body leaned into me.

My arms looped around her waist, bringing her as close as humanly possible. A little sound escaped her lips, which nearly took me over the edge.

She mouth parted more, tasting as sweet as ever. Her tongue invited me into her mouth, swirling and playfully teasing me. Emily's hands slowly worked up my spine. Her fingernails slid along my scalp, tangling in my hair.

Emily's mouth pressed even harder against mine as she nipped at my bottom lip before sliding her tongue along my lips as I welcomed her into this temporary bliss.

That was the thing with Emily. I didn't know what she wanted because she didn't even know what she wanted, and this right here.

Proved that.

As I held her in my arms and my pulse raced with need and excitement, I couldn't help but wonder if this would be the last time we shared a kiss.

Again.

Because I was ready to love her with everything I had in me.

But I didn't know if she understood that.

Or even felt the same.

Her curvy body fit into mine so well.

It was impossible not to imagine her naked, fitting into me as only Emily could. The thought nearly undid me as I held her in my arms, our kisses only deepening with every passing second, every gust of the wind.

For just a moment, I let myself pretend that this could go somewhere. That maybe she'd let us take that next step.

And then Emily's kisses slowed, her mouth parted from mine, and she rested her head on my chest.

"You bring it out of me," she whispered, bringing her eyes to mine. "I'm sorry. That wasn't nice of me. I'm sending mixed messages."

I laughed, brushing some hair from her forehead. "That was very nice of you."

She giggled, and the sound lit up my world.

Her green eyes stayed focused on mine, and the heat firing behind her gaze only stirred the wildness inside me.

Our eyes stayed locked on one another as I cupped her face in my hands and kissed her again, and this time, I wasn't holding back. My mouth teased her lips, moving to her neck, feeling the softness of her skin as my breath skated across it.

Emily arched her back as I pulled her curvy hips into me and the rawness of my need was no longer hidden.

I let myself believe that circumstances were different as our kisses intensified and her breath hitched with the same desire I felt.

A car horn honked, breaking us apart, and Emily's gaze landed on Amelia and James's vehicle as it slowed down.

Amelia rolled down the window and waved. "About damn time."

Chapter Fifteen

Emily

"You look absolutely rosy and bright," Mimi said, eyeing me with a twinkle in her eyes. "I recognize that flush."

I straightened in the dining room chair as I scooped mashed potatoes onto her plate. "I don't know what you're talking about."

Mimi chuckled. "Right, of course. You don't have a thing to say about anything."

I glanced at my grandpa, who was staring at the roast chicken on his plate, holding in a chuckle.

"Very funny, you two."

Turning my attention back to Mimi, I drizzled gravy on her plate and handed it over.

"You might not have anything to say, but that

hickey on your neck says otherwise." It was like she just couldn't contain herself. Mimi chuckled as my hand slapped the side of my neck where Lucas's lips were just yesterday.

"I..." Taking a bite of chicken, I stared at my grandma and swallowed. "I don't know what I was thinking."

"Maybe that's the problem. You think too much." Mimi cast a glance at me before looking at my grandpa. "If you overthink love, it becomes too complicated."

"Love?" I spat out. "I'm not in love."

"From all accounts, you've been going back and forth with him for a year. I'm surprised he's stuck around this long."

I futzed around with my napkin on my lap. "We're just friends, Mimi. I messed up and kissed him. My fault. He completely understands. Problem solved."

"You know that your other Grandma and I didn't particularly get along, right?"

This was something we all knew and pretended wasn't the case. Mimi was more outspoken, while

Grandma Cecilia thought carefully about words.

Meanings.

Implications.

They argued a lot when they were younger, or so I heard, but by the time we grandkids were old enough to notice, they'd ironed out their differences.

"But the one thing we agreed on wholeheartedly was you, our little wildflower." She took a sip of wine. "You are patient like a wildflower, waiting for just the right conditions. Even when you were a child. You'd watch your siblings squabble and wait for them to hash things out before you got involved. You'd think with your heart, not your head with them."

"I suppose that's true." I nodded.

"But you never ignored your heart, either, and that is something I don't want you to forget. If you cut that off, you have nothing but a mind that sees only logic."

I stared at her, unsure where she was going with this analogy.

"And logic will talk you out of things that could be quite good for the heart."

A smile touched my lips.

"The wilds of the heart are a special thing. Listen to these whispers. Let those whispers become shouts when it's a matter of the heart."

"That's true," my grandpa agreed.

"It's okay to go a little crazy, do wild things. You've never let things stop you before." She smiled at me. "I know I'm your grandma, and you probably don't want to take advice on your love life from an old lady."

"Not true," I assured her.

"But what's the worst that could happen if you listened to your heart instead of your head?"

I sat quietly for a few seconds.

She tried again. "It's like with your poetry. It's beautiful. It's from the heart." She tapped her chest. "It's raw and vulnerable."

I stared at my Mimi, wondering how she knew anything about my poetry.

She smiled and tipped her chin toward the living room. "You left a copy tucked in the chair. You're very talented."

My cheeks warmed. "Thank you. It's kind of a

secret."

"Those words on that paper are freer than anything I've seen come out of your mouth in a long time." She glanced at her husband and then back at me. "Don't let life wear you down before you've had a chance to live it fully."

"But I could lose a friend, or I could get my heart broken beyond repair, or both."

"Maybe you've already crossed that bridge," Mimi suggested. "But what if you have something so special and resilient at your fingertips but you lose it?"

I sighed and pushed around my chicken. Mimi was right.

It had been two days since our kiss near the beach. I'd texted him a couple of times, and he texted back. I was trying extremely hard not to fold up into my cocoon and ignore him like last time.

And he was still on Marigold.

I looked down at my food and smiled. "I think I'll wrap this up and save it for later."

Mimi looked pleased and nodded. "Good idea."

I made my way to the kitchen, wrapped plastic

wrap over the plate, and found a spot to prop it in the fridge before texting Lucas.

How's Oscar?

He wrote back almost instantly.

Could be better.

I tapped my foot and brought in a breath.

Would you be into some company?
My phone buzzed.

I would be nuts to turn you down. My sister stopped by, but she's leaving.

Maybe things would be okay. I couldn't slide the smile off my face as I grabbed my keys and popped my head back into the dining room to say goodbye.

Mimi's eyes connected with mine, and she waggled her brows. "We won't wait up."

I winced and shook my head. "Mimi."

My grandpa chuckled, and I walked out the front door, wondering why I had to have this revelation with my grandparents staying at my house.

Of all times.

As I put on my helmet and climbed on the scooter, excitement tinged every thought. One second, I thought about kissing him right when he answered. The other, I imagined him taking me into his arms and…

I shook my head and laughed, realizing I needed to take things one step at a time.

Especially with Oscar around.

Besides, a kiss at the beach didn't automatically change everything.

Or did it?

All I knew was by the time I pulled through the gates of his family's orchard, I was a jumbled mess of emotions.

As the breeze blew along my skin, I let out a deep breath and nodded, pulling to a stop in front of the main house. I spotted his sister's car still parked in front of the garage.

I climbed off the scooter and made my way to the front door that was open. Hopefully, Oscar hadn't snuck out. Or maybe that was Lucas's hope. I hid in a chuckle and called a *Hello* out.

No answer.

I walked into the grand foyer with lavish molding, tall ceilings, and very ornate furniture. It kind of felt like a time capsule of when his grandparents lived here.

"Hello," I called out again.

I heard soft murmurs down the hall and made my way when I heard Nina.

"It's not surprising the emotions resurfaced despite all your efforts to keep them away," Nina said sympathetically.

Clara.

My stomach clenched, and I wanted to back out of the hallway silently, but I couldn't help myself as I strained to hear.

"But the history there isn't..." He cleared his throat. "I just don't know if it will make things worse or if I just have to accept that I want something I shouldn't have."

My jaw tightened as I stared at the wall of paintings and photos. Taking a deep breath, I let it out slowly and told myself it was going to be fine. Everything would be fine.

We'd still be friends. I'd have him in my life. We wouldn't be doing this back and forth.

I blinked my eyes open and tried again. "Hello, guys." I dipped my head into the gathering room where Lucas gave a quick welcome in as Nina smiled at me.

She touched her brother's arm and nodded. "We'll talk more."

"I think I'm all talked out." He hugged Nina, and she started toward the hall and then stopped abruptly.

"Hey, did you come up with anyone to bring to Mom and Dad's anniversary party?" She eyed her brother.

First I'd heard of it. Maybe he'd hoped to invite Clara.

Lucas laughed and looked over at me. "Matter of fact, I wanted to ask Emily." His eyes locked on mine, and confusion settled in. "My parents decided on an impromptu anniversary celebration, complete with vow renewals. Would you care to be my date?"

My heart skipped a beat as Nina waved goodbye and let herself out. I heard the door close behind her and looked around. The gathering room overlooked the water. A grand brick fireplace stretched to the ceiling, and the flames roiled. The classic furniture fit the style of the rest of the house, and I assumed it had been untouched.

"When is it?" I asked.

"Two days from now."

I frowned. "I don't have anything to wear."

"That's an easy fix," Lucas said. "So, is that a yes?"

I bit my bottom lip and thought about it, remembering my mission when I came over here.

"Sure." I nodded. "Yeah. That sounds fun."

But I could feel my guard going up around my heart, piece by piece, again.

Lucas looped his arms around me and pulled me in. "Thank goodness. I was worried I'd have to show up solo."

"God forbid," I whispered.

"You have no idea." He laughed. "My parents want us to dance with them."

My eyes flashed to his. "I have two left feet. Like, I'm really awful."

"Just let me lead," he said, taking a step back.

But he didn't let go. He slid his hand into mine, wrapped his other arm around my waist, and started to glide with me in his arms.

"This is the foxtrot," he said, his voice low. "It should work for whatever they have planned."

I glanced down, trying to copy his feet, but he shook his head. "Keep your eyes on me and let me guide you. Your feet will have no choice but to follow."

Laughing nervously, I kept my eyes on his. "If you say so."

His smile only widened as his feet moved in a rhythm of his making. To my surprise, I was keeping up, not stepping on his feet or getting mine squashed.

"See?" His voice grumbled deep into my belly, and I couldn't help but get turned on.

"This is a first," I confessed. "Usually, one of us

would wind up limping at the end."

He laughed, pulling me in close. "We just fit in so many ways, Emily."

Our steps slowed, and his eyes stayed on mine.

"That's why I came over," I said softly. "I need to start listening to my heart."

"And what does your heart say?" he asked, tipping my chin up toward his.

I tried to push away the conversation between his sister and him and focused on my mission.

"To give us a try."

He stood as still as stone and didn't take his eyes off me.

"I'm too late," I said softly.

Lucas cocked his head as his blue eyes flickered with something raw. "Too late for what?"

"Us?" I cleared my throat and looked around for Oscar, trying to save face. "I hate to ask this, but where's the cat?"

Lucas scowled. "He attacked my foot. Thank God I had hiking boots on, so he's in a timeout."

I looked around. "Where at? Inside the

fireplace?"

"No. I'm not sadistic. He's in one of the guest bedrooms with plenty of food, water, and litter." He touched my chin softly, bringing my gaze back to his. "But why would you think you're too late? Don't try to change the topic."

He was on to me.

I didn't even want to utter her name at this point. Maybe it was all in my head. I didn't even know.

"Just because it took me a while." I twisted my lips into a pout. "To get my head on straight."

"I would have waited a lifetime, Emily." He smiled, bringing his hands to my face. "But I'm glad I didn't have to."

His mouth sealed over mine, lips so soft. My eyes closed as his tongue parted my mouth, feeling every single moment. Lucas slid his hands under my shirt. His fingers glided easily over my bare skin. Heat pooled deep in my belly as I realized I wouldn't stop him, no matter how far we went.

Lucas's tongue stroked mine, swirling and teasing me with such expertise as his hands unfastened my bra. I let out a little moan of happiness as he pulled off my shirt, only breaking the kiss long enough to move it over my head. I wiggled the bra off before I slid my hands under his shirt, feeling the hardness of his stomach.

I could feel his length pressing into me as my knees weakened with anticipation. My breathing quickened with every lash of his tongue as he worked his kisses along my collarbone and down to my breasts.

Lucas kneeled in front of me, cupping one breast with his palm while he used his mouth over the other breast, teasing my nipple with every flick of his tongue.

My fingers tangled through his hair as he unbuttoned my jeans and kept teasing me with his mouth.

"Lucas," I said breathlessly.

He looked up at me, smiling. "Should I stop?"

I shook my head. "But I can't keep standing."

Lucas let out a low, deep growl as he scooped me into his arms and placed me on the couch, pulling down my jeans. He pulled his shirt off as I motioned for him to unzip his pants, which he quickly kicked off.

I had no idea his body was so insane. His eyes

locked on mine as my breath caught in my throat. He knelt down, moving his mouth over my underwear. The heat from his breath created a frenzy inside as I twisted my fingers through his hair. He brought his eyes to mine and smiled as he slowly worked my underwear down, kissing the exposed skin as he went.

He reached his hand to my breasts again while moving his other hand across my belly, moving lower until he pushed his fingers inside me.

I let out a gasp as I felt him slide inside me, never taking his eyes from mine. I braced myself as the rhythm of his hand made my entire body move up and down.

"God, you're so sexy." His voice was low and gravelly as my body tightened with need.

My breathing turned to panting as his gaze stayed fastened on mine.

"Good girl," he murmured as I bit my lip and threw my head back in absolute ecstasy. Wave after wave rippled through me as he climbed on top of me, caging me in with his arms and kissing me like I'd never been kissed before.

"I'm not done with you," he whispered as my

body still shuddered against his.

I could feel the length of him resting on my belly as his eyes locked on mine, and I nodded, needing so much more.

He nudged my knees wider as his mouth slid along my neck, and he slid into me. I'd never felt so much inside me. My body tensed as he slowly eased in, bringing his gaze back to mine.

"You okay?"

I nodded, moving my hands along his spine. "More than okay. Please don't stop."

Feeling him inside me brought a closeness that I never knew possible as he thrust deeper.

With every push, my world spun out of control, and my heart took over as our bodies exploded with all the need and longing we'd ignored for so long.

He held me in his arms as I tried to catch my breath, feeling his heart hammer in his chest. "I think I'm falling in love with you, Lucas."

"I'm already there," he said softly.

My eyes locked on his, and I drew a breath. "Now what?"

"We're just getting started," he whispered as his mouth crashed down to mine.

Chapter Sixteen

Lucas

She woke up in my arms this morning, and it was the most amazing feeling I'd ever experienced in my life. I curled my arm around her head as she nestled into the soft pillow, pressing her body into mine as she let out a little murmur. Her eyes slowly opened, and her gaze connected with mine.

"Morning," I whispered, brushing a kiss along her cheek.

"Is this a dream?" she asked, turning over to look at me.

Her dark hair framed her face as she stretched her arms and let out a low hum. I could see doing this for the rest of my life.

I hoped I'd get the chance.

"Thank goodness you didn't ask if it was a nightmare." I laughed, and she cuddled into me.

"There is one part that isn't great about it." She cupped her hands onto my chest and pushed back a little as a smile lined her perfect mouth.

"What's that?" With Emily, I never knew.

"My grandparents are at my house and they know I never made it home last night." She groaned, pushing her hand to her forehead. "I'll never hear the end of this."

"Nah, I can't imagine it will be that bad," I assured her.

She snickered. "We'll see." Turning on her side, she traced her finger along my chest. "But, do you know what Mimi said to me when I left yesterday?"

I laughed, propping my head on my hand and shaking my head.

Emily's gaze locked on mine and filled with mischief. "She said *we won't wait up*." She shuddered.

I pulled her head in and kissed it playfully. "Good thing they didn't."

"What time is it?" she asked, sitting up slowly and stretching again.

"Almost eight o'clock." She yawned and stretched toward the ceiling. It was impossible to take my eyes off her. "Good. I have time to go home, shower, and change."

I crawled next to her and slowly massaged her bare shoulders. "You could shower here."

Emily laughed and shook her head, turning to face me. "You and I both know I would never make it to work." She traced her index finger along my jaw and placed a quick kiss on my nose. "You're kind of addictive."

"I like the sound of that." I nuzzled my nose with hers. "I was thinking intoxicating."

She chuckled and nodded. "That too."

Emily stood, and the curves of her body made me hard again. I pulled the sheet around me and got off the bed. Just seeing her made my breath quicken.

"While you get dressed, I'm going to shower really quick. How about I drive you to your house? It's pretty cold to get on your scooter."

Her eyes traced along my body, and she smiled. "Suddenly modest?"

"No. Just don't want to have you distracted at the store all day."

"I dare you to drop the sheet," she teased.

"It's not much of a dare, Emily. I'd have you again in a second."

Her cheeks flushed as she pulled on her underwear, and I ripped my gaze from her, making my way to the bathroom.

Turning on the shower, I let the steam fill up the room as I looked in the mirror.

It was kind of crazy, but I felt completely different… like the person looking back at me no longer had a care in the world.

I stepped into the shower and watched Emily walk into the room. She found some toothpaste, squirted it onto her finger, and started brushing.

She spun around and looked through the steamy glass as suds covered my body. Just like that, I imagined us married, caught up in our morning routine, and my heart filled with actual joy.

As the water trickled over my body, rinsing off the soap, she bent over and finished with her teeth. I knew with certainty that there wasn't another woman in the world whom I'd want like her.

Ever.

I turned off the shower, wrapping a white towel around me as I stepped onto the tile.

"I'll go check on Oscar."

"Be careful. He's roaming around somewhere. I opened the door last night after you fell asleep."

She playfully grimaced and nodded. "I'll be extra careful. Meet you in the kitchen? I'll get coffee started."

I nodded, sliding the towel along my legs as I watched Emily walk away.

It was taking everything I had to not make love to her again. Everything about last night was sensational.

Emily was sensational.

My phone buzzed, and I glanced at it on the bathroom counter. My cousin's face showed up, and I had to laugh.

He never texted this early.

I rubbed the towel over my head and wrapped it around my body as I glanced at the message.

Congratulations. Amelia said they all agreed she could have the day off.

I laughed, shaking my head. She would kill them. It had to be Mimi. I smiled, texting back. I certainly wasn't going to confess.

I don't know what you're talking about, but do you want to have lunch later?

My cousin didn't text back, so I walked to the closet, pulled on a pair of jeans, tugged on a T-shirt, and stuffed my phone in my back pocket. It still felt weird not having my grandparents here. It had been years, but there were moments when I thought they'd suddenly appear. We'd all done our best at keeping the house pretty much how they'd left it. My parents had some things in the primary bedroom, and Nina and I each took a spare room for those times when we felt like staying on Marigold.

"Oscar, bad kitty. Bad kitty," Emily's voice echoed through the house.

Oh, no. That couldn't be good.

I dashed out of the bedroom and beelined toward Emily's voice. She was kneeling down near a Ficus that no longer stood tall. Dirt spilled onto the wood floors and several branches had snapped.

She looked at me. "I am so sorry."

"Don't be. It's one less plant for the caretakers."

Emily's chin tilted. "You have a caretaker?"

I nodded, waving my hand around at the various plants. "We aren't here enough to take care of everything, and I can barely keep my own plant alive at home."

I made my way down the hall to the pantry, where a broom was stored.

"Besides, you have nothing to apologize for. It's Brad's cat." I smiled at her as she glared at Oscar.

"Here, let me do it." She reached for the broom, but I moved it away.

"I got it." I smiled, shaking my head. "Don't give it a second thought."

"At least I got the coffee started."

I moved the pot upright, and the tree had a lean

to it, and I chuckled. "That will give my parents something to talk about."

Her eyes widened, and she gasped. "Oh, no."

"Kidding." I shook my head, taking the dirt to the trash.

She was right behind me as I put the broom into the pantry. "Wow. This pantry is bigger than my kitchen."

"Size isn't everything," I joked.

"I don't know. After last night, I'd say it's something of a factor."

I burst into laughter as she moved her arms around my waist from behind. "That was a really big surprise."

Shaking my head, I turned to face her and kissed her forehead. "Are you telling me had you known about that, you might have given in a little sooner?"

She giggled and gave me a hug as the coffeemaker beeped.

"Good things come to those who wait, right?" She grinned, looping her fingers through mine as we made our way into the kitchen. I got two travel mugs from the cabinet and poured our coffee, securing the lids.

"Are you sure you don't mind driving me home and to the store?"

I shook my head. "It gives me a reason to see you more."

She took a sip of coffee and let out a low hum of satisfaction.

Damn, everything about her was a turn-on.

She glanced at the clock and back at me. "We should probably get going. I'm pretty speedy at getting ready, but I think Audrey's out today, so I don't want to leave them hanging."

"Totally." I nodded, remembering my cousin's text.

As I grabbed the keys and my wallet and we made our way to my car, I debated about warning her. It was the right thing to do.

When we climbed inside, she turned on the radio and happily sipped the coffee.

"I got a text from my cousin this morning bright and early."

She glanced over at me. "Oh, yeah?"

I nodded. "Seems that Mimi has already informed your sisters that you didn't come home last night."

Emily chuckled and then groaned as she propped her head into her hands. "Doesn't this seem strange? Like, are all grandparents this nosy?"

I laughed, shaking my head. "You got me there. My family has the opposite problem. We barely communicate. Everyone is always running in their own directions."

"Oh, geez. That's kind of sad." She turned to look at me.

"Yeah, I guess it could be, but it's how I grew up. I know my parents love me. There's no doubt there, and they did an amazing job providing support for my cousin too." I cleared my throat and shrugged. "But it's just not… tight. You know?"

"You mean everybody's business isn't the topic of every conversation?" she joked, putting her hand on my knee.

"Something like that." I eyed Emily and wondered how we'd finally made it to this point. Things felt so good… amazing.

And it was almost easy enough to forget that there was a possibility that she could be leaving for three months.

"I just can't believe I'm about to do the walk of shame at my own house in front of my grandparents. Isn't she going to be embarrassed knowing her granddaughter…"

"That'll teach her to break a hip," I teased. "But if you don't mind, I'll just wait out here."

Emily laughed and nodded. "I wouldn't dream of having it any other way. Believe me."

I pulled up in front of her bungalow, and she started to climb out of her car, but I grabbed her wrist and brought her in for a kiss.

It felt so good, knowing I didn't have to pretend any longer.

"I'll be waiting," I told her.

She smiled and planted another kiss on my mouth before she got out of the car.

I turned on some music and sat back in the seat, closing my eyes as last night ran through my brain.

Spending last night with Emily was incredible, and she didn't seem to be shutting down or clamming up so far, which was what I'd been worried about.

But the poetry residency kept going through my mind, too. Three months was a long time, and I would have no problem waiting for her to return. My only hope would be that she would come back.

A tap on my window surprised me, and I opened my eyes to see her grandpa peering through the window with a cup of coffee.

I rolled down the window and smiled. "Good morning."

"Especially for some, heh?" He leaned against the car and nodded, looking toward the horizon.

I didn't know what to say, so I stayed quiet and tried not to laugh. Now, I understood what she meant when everyone was in everyone's business.

"How are things?" her grandpa asked.

I nodded, smiling. "Things are going well."

"Good. Good." He brought his eyes back to me.

"I hope you know that I treasure your granddaughter."

"Oh, I have no doubt that you do." He nodded and straightened, taking a sip of coffee. "But I wanted to warn you."

I glanced toward the bungalow.

Oh, no. Not the shotgun talk. I'd always despised that concept.

He lowered his head so I would be sure to hear him. "She's a flight risk."

"Pardon?"

He pressed his thin lips together and nodded sympathetically. "Her grandmother was like that too, and I recognize the similarities."

"Oh," was all I said since my mind drew a blank.

"There is this impulsive quality about them. Mimi likes to think of herself as more pragmatic, less mystical than the other side of the family. But truth be told, she's more damn spiritual than any of them. She doesn't even cut flowers out of her garden for fear of hurting them."

I laughed, shaking my head. Mimi always struck me as no-nonsense. The thought that she was kind to a rose puzzled me.

"Some people call it a gut feeling, other people say intuition." He shook his head and let out a deep breath. "They run on that feeling, and if something feels even a little different, they are out like a shot. Notice I said different, not bad. Just different. They put meaning to every single thing. That can be good, or it can be awful. I almost lost Mimi when I was nineteen because she had a funny feeling." He scratched his head. "Come to find out, it was love."

I nodded, feeling the unsettling sensation in my stomach at the thought of the residency.

He reached in and patted my shoulder. "Just be prepared to chase after her. That's all I'm saying."

I laughed nervously as I saw Emily bounding out of the house wearing an orange sundress. "Thanks. I appreciate it."

"Absolutely. I'm here to lend an ear."

I gave a quick nod as her grandpa backed away, and she opened the door. "Whew. Record time. I've got frozen lasagna defrosting in the fridge for lunch, Grandpa."

He chuckled and nodded with a quick wave.

"Keep this up, and we might never go home."

We pulled away, and she laughed. "And that is what I'm terrified of."

Chapter Seventeen

Emily

I took a bite of a coconut macaroon and sipped on a mocha while sitting at a table at Mae's. She was going over some things with one of her employees, but she promised to come dress shopping with me down the street.

Come to think of it, I probably shouldn't be slamming a thousand calories for my snack before trying on slinky dresses.

Not that Lucas hadn't seen every inch of me.

Ah, who cares?

It still felt like a dream. We'd crossed that bridge, and everything about it felt... right. There were no nagging little feelings or uneasiness roaring to life. It was refreshing. And I hadn't hidden in a corner, ignoring his

241

texts and pretending it didn't happen, so I'd say that was a step in the right direction.

Not that I could ever forget that it happened. The man was skilled. I shook my head, taking a bite of macaroon as I dreamily thought back to his expert hands.

"Are we going or what?" Mae asked, slipping her hands to her hips. "It's like the third time I've asked."

I shot up from the chair and popped the last bit of coconut into my mouth and smiled. "Sorry. I'm out of it."

Mae's brow arched, and a smirk rested on her features. "Believe me, I've heard."

I chuckled, dabbing my lips with a napkin before tossing it in the trash on the way outside. "I don't know who has heard what, other than to say that all day, my entire family has been giving me side eye. It's kind of creepy."

Mae laughed as we walked down the sidewalk. "I don't know. Mimi called Mom."

"What? Mom? Ew."

"She only said that you didn't come home last night and wondered if she should be worried." Mae laughed. "Mom saw right through it."

"Yet, she felt compelled to share with you," I pointed out with a laugh.

"Yeah. I can tell you if I ever find the man of my dreams, I'm just going to show up already eloped."

I stole a look at Mae, wondering if she ever seriously thought about dating.

"So, is it true...?" Her voice trailed off, and she smiled at me.

I couldn't hide my grin and nodded. "Yeah."

"Finally. Amelia said she saw you two playing tonsil hockey at the beach, so I held out hope that you'd finally just go for it."

I chuckled as we landed at the dress boutique. "Yeah?"

"Yup. You only live once."

I opened the door. "I'll have to remember that."

The store was super cute and full of every kind of dress imaginable, but with prom season only a couple of months away, it felt like a glitter bonanza.

"Oooh. Wow." Mae's hand caressed a pink sequined dress. "This would say something for sure."

I giggled and nodded. "That I'm homecoming queen?"

I scanned the store, finally landing on a section not geared toward seventeen-year-olds and made my way over with Mae right behind me.

Gianna, who was the daughter of the woman who owned the store, stepped out from behind the counter and waved.

"Hi, Ladies." She beamed, walking over to us. "Anything I can help you find?"

"I'm going to an anniversary party over in Seattle."

"Oh, fun." Gianna nodded. "Is it black tie or…?"

"I got that impression."

"It's with Lucas Edwards," my sister piped in, and my cheeks blushed.

Gianna's eyes widened. "Oh, then you definitely need formal."

I nodded in agreement as her hands swept over an ivory, beaded lace dress.

"This would be stunning." She took the hanger off the rack and held it up. "It's hard to tell, but this plunges nicely in the front without being too revealing, but the surprise is in the back."

She spun it around to show off the backless dress.

"You always look spectacular in mermaid fits," Mae said, sliding her hand over the beadwork.

"It's all hand-sewn," Gianna said as I glanced at the price tag.

I held in a whistle, but I could see why it cost so much. It was beautiful.

"What do you say? Do you want to try it on?" Gianna asked.

I glanced at my sister and then nodded.

"Perfect. Right this way."

I followed Gianna into the back where the fitting rooms were as she hung the dress up on a hook, and I stepped inside.

"I'll be out here if you need me."

"Thank you," I told her, closing the curtain before staring at the dress.

My hand moved along the beadwork, and I couldn't help but fall in love with it a little more.

I pulled my sundress over my head and folded it

on a chair before pulling the gown off the hanger. My fingers worked the buttons and zipper and I gingerly slid into the gown. The silky fabric glided across my skin.

I glanced in the mirror and was taken aback. A chill ran through me as I noticed the fabric clinging to my curves. I worked the zipper up and finagled the buttons while staring at myself in the mirror.

"Well?" Mae asked outside the curtain.

"It's gorgeous, but it's almost too perfect for a wedding… as in I'd be the bride."

I turned around and opened the curtain to see Mae light up.

"You are gorgeous. You have to get this." She reached out and ran her fingers along my left side. "It hugs you in all the right places."

I nodded, grateful she thought it looked great too.

"But I do see how it hints at bridal."

"Maybe it could be two birds with one stone."

Mae's brows rose. "With Lucas?"

I nodded, feeling my cheeks flush.

She let out a deep breath and glanced over her shoulder before walking into the dressing room with me.

Mae closed the curtain.

"What's up?"

"Are you serious about that?"

I frowned and shook my head, bewildered. "Well, it's a little early on in the whole relationship. I was only teasing."

Her expression didn't change much. "What happened to him always going out on dates? You always told me he was busy every weekend. Has he just stopped all of a sudden?"

Her question was one that had flittered through my mind a time or two.

"The last few weeks, he hasn't been on any that I know of."

Her brows arched. "And how long do you think that will last?"

I chuckled nervously, touching my chest. "I'd like to believe for as long as I'm with him."

She nodded in silence. "Aren't you worried about his past?"

Agitation tickled its way through me as I stared at my sister. This was supposed to be a fun outing, but I couldn't be mad at her. She wasn't coming from a vicious place. I'd spent the entire year proclaiming to the world that Lucas wasn't the settling down type and that I could never be fooled by his antics.

And then I slept with him.

Worse yet, I let myself dream of a future with him.

"I get it, and I've definitely been torn about jumping into this with him, but I'm leading with my heart, not my head this time."

She nodded. "That's what scares me."

"But I'm also still guarded. I..." I shrugged. "I just want to try."

"I understand." She smiled. "I really do, because not trying would make you live wondering if you missed out on something great. At least this way, you'll know one way or another."

I nodded, knowing my sister wasn't just talking about me. She never got to know. I took a step back and smiled. "Okay. So, what do you think? A winner?"

My sister grinned. "Absolutely. And if he doesn't treat you right, he has your siblings to deal with."

I chuckled, nodding. "Not to mention Mimi."

My sister pretended to shiver as I worked the dress off me.

I placed it back on the hanger and got dressed quickly. Even though I was still excited about the party, hearing my sister's concerns recharged mine.

But that was the problem with me and why I couldn't let myself imagine something more with Lucas. I was scared, and like she said, at least I'd know.

I pushed the thoughts aside, and my sister caught my gaze. "I didn't mean to be a downer. I'm seriously happy for you."

"No, I know. These aren't things that haven't run through my mind." I shrugged, grabbing the dress. "It's why it's taken me so long to finally agree to move past the friend zone."

She squeezed me. "Okay, because I love you, and I'm super excited for you. And if you believe in him, I believe in him."

As I paid for the dress, my sister left the store to return to her coffee shop. There was a little pit in the bottom of my stomach, and I didn't like it one bit. I'd come off a high of Lucas to a sounding board of worry.

I signed the receipt and thanked Gianna before I headed out the door. I'd have to hang the gown upstairs until Lucas came to pick me up.

The thought of seeing him again instantly lifted my spirits as I walked into our store.

I glanced at the statue of Artemis that my mom touched every single day before she left the store. She was certain that her mom's spirit somehow lived on through that sculpture. It was a nice thought, but the problem was that sometimes, the romantic idea of something made the reality a letdown. What if the statue broke? Then what? Did that mean her mom no longer existed to feel?

What if Lucas broke my heart? I wanted to believe our reality could be as magical as it felt, but I'd be lying to myself if I wasn't still a little worried.

I marched up the stairs of the antique store and hung my dress up, giving it one more glance before I left. It was exciting to think I actually had somewhere to wear it.

As I turned around, I nearly ran over my mom.

"That's a beautiful dress, Emily." She sipped a latte from Mae's café. "And your sister feels awful for bombarding you about Lucas."

I shook my head. "No, she's fine. I get it. I've been navigating through the same stuff."

But I knew by the look in Lucas's gaze that he wouldn't hurt me, not intentionally.

She touched my cheek and smiled. "I'm so proud of you."

Surprise registered over my expression. "Why?"

"Because you're listening to your heart again." She gave a little squeeze on my arm. "Don't stop. It's what makes you special, and it's never guided you astray."

I chuckled and let out a deep breath. "We shall see."

My mom tapped her chest. "Good things will come. He's a great guy. So, where are you going that you need a dress like that?"

"His parents are having an anniversary party and renewing their vows. It's in Seattle, and I got the impression that it's kind of swanky."

She chuckled. "Knowing the Edwards family, I'm sure it is."

"I've only met his parents a few times, but they've always seemed nice."

"They are." My mom nodded, and the bell below dinged. "You'll win them over."

"I hope so."

She took a seat at her desk while I went downstairs to see if Amelia needed any help with the customers.

But for some reason, a pesky little voice started nipping in my ear, and it was about Clara. Was that who Nina was talking about with Lucas? Or was my imagination just running wild? I let out a quiet groan. I'd never been a jealous person, and I certainly didn't want to start now. However, the thought occurred to me about the timing of things. I didn't want to be a prize to be had, all because I'd played the game right.

The more I thought about it, the more I wondered if I'd flirted with Lucas right away, if he would have given me a second glance. Instead, I let him and his cousin have it about how they'd treated my sister. The thought brought a smile to my lips.

Yeah, I'd be fine no matter how this ended. I was resilient and wouldn't let him play with my heart.

Chapter Eighteen

Lucas

Emily took my breath away. The beaded ivory dress clung to Emily's curves and left little to the imagination.

"Spin for me," I said softly, taking her in.

She chuckled, rolled her eyes, and turned around slowly.

The gown flowed like a sculptural masterpiece as her eyes met mine. "You approve?"

I couldn't wipe the grin off my face as I pulled her into me and kissed her.

A warm and affectionate giggle fell from her lips as she pulled away and glanced at her sister.

James and Amelia drove Emily over to my place in the city, and we were all going to leave together for the party.

But it was like they weren't even here. Emily gave me tunnel vision.

"Should we get going?" James asked, glancing at his phone. "The car is waiting downstairs."

"Sounds good." I reached for my tuxedo jacket and slid it on as Emily's eyes lit up in satisfaction.

James and Amelia were already headed back toward the elevator bank as Emily stared at me.

"You clean up nice," she said, running her fingers along my lapel.

"Every once in a while, I can trade jeans for this."

Emily slid a kiss across my cheek before I locked the door behind me.

I ran my hands along her spine, feeling her bare skin underneath my fingertips. If it weren't for it being my parents' party, I'd turn us around and stay in bed all night.

The elevator chimed, and we all stepped inside.

"You ready to dance in front of everyone tonight?" her sister teased.

I laughed, keeping my hand on her back for

reassurance. "Believe it or not, Emily and I have been practicing, and she's amazing at the fox trot."

"Okay. I'm impressed." Amelia chuckled as the carriage opened on the main floor and we walked into the lobby.

The waiting SUV was already at the curb, and we all wandered outside to feel a gentle nip in the air.

"Spring is having a hard time making up its mind," James muttered as he opened the car door for all of us.

"I'll get in first since my dress is less restrictive," Amelia joked, climbing inside as James helped her.

Emily glanced at me and whispered *love you* as she crawled up into the SUV, holding my hand as she teetered on the edge.

"This isn't the most practical dress." She laughed, trying to squirm into the seat as I got in after her.

"I could breathe in it just fine earlier, but now it feels like I need to get rid of a rib or something." She sucked in a breath and looked at me with the seatbelt in her hand. "Could you?"

I nodded and reached over, buckling her in as she thanked me and the driver pulled into traffic.

"So, your parents are renewing their vows?" my cousin asked, knowing the answer. "Doesn't that jinx things?"

I laughed. "I've heard that, but I don't think my parents are going anywhere. They like bickering with each other too much."

James laughed. "Indeed. And nine times out of ten, they agree about it the entire time they're bickering."

"Yeah. I don't get it."

"Maybe there's something to that," Amelia offered, leaning forward and tapping Emily's shoulder. "You were always giving Lucas a hard time until recently."

Emily grinned. "I've softened slightly toward him."

"I have that effect on people."

"What was it you said?" James joked. "Your plan was to just wear Emily down?"

I snuck a look in Emily's direction, and surprise washed over her face.

"Wear me down, huh? How do you know I wasn't just wearing *you* down?" She flashed a wry grin. "Maybe that was my plan all along."

I reached for her hand and held it in mine. "Well, whatever happened, it worked."

Emily laughed, and the sound was better than anything the driver could have had on the radio.

I saw the tower come into view as the driver pulled in front to let us out.

Emily looked over at me. "I think if I twist wrong, beads will start exploding from this thing."

I chuckled and nodded.

"Thank you so much for getting us here safe and sound," I told the driver as I helped unbuckle Emily.

He gave a quick nod. "My pleasure."

I opened the door, got out of the car, and helped Emily wiggle out in her dress.

We made our way to the towering building. My parents had rented out the top floor so there'd be a beautiful view of the city to accompany the dinner and dancing.

Amelia and James were behind us as the doorman

welcomed us inside and directed us to the elevators.

The ride up was quiet, and I sensed Emily getting nervous, which killed me. She was perfection. She had nothing to be worried about.

The carriage doors opened into a grand ballroom that glittered with opulence. The crystal chandelier cast a soft glow on the tables underneath, which were adorned with enormous floral arrangements.

"How did your parents pull this off in a matter of weeks?"

I laughed, shaking my head as I scanned the room that had already filled with friends, family, and my parents' coworkers.

Emily and I stood at the entrance while James and Amelia walked toward the open bar.

"You ready?" I asked.

"My heart is racing," she said softly, looking into my eyes.

I leaned down and swept a soft kiss across her lips. "You have nothing to be worried about. My parents will love you, and they already know you."

Her smile grew as she ran her fingers along her

hips.

"This feels like a fairytale," Emily whispered as I cupped my hand around hers.

"We'd better find my parents," I said, tightening my grip around hers.

As Emily made her way through the crowd with me, her gown shimmered from the lights above. She was a masterpiece.

The delicate embroidery weaving together the beadwork paired with the exotic lace was magnificent. She'd styled her hair into a braided crown with a few strands framing her delicate features.

"You look like an angel," I whispered.

She turned to look at me and cocked her head slightly. "Thank you for always making me feel so beautiful."

"Well, you are," I whispered.

My eyes fell to her mouth, but just as I was about to lean down to kiss her, I heard my mom's voice echo through the ballroom.

"There you are, Lucas. Nina hasn't even left her place yet. Can you believe your sister?"

The crowd parted for my mom as she glided across the ballroom floor as if she owned the place.

Her silver dress shimmered like a snakeskin as she made her way over to us with my father right behind.

My mom immediately recognized Emily and smiled, clapping her hands. "Oh, I'm so glad you could make it tonight, Emily. You're one of the few people who can keep him in line."

Emily chuckled and nodded. "I try my best, but he's a handful."

My mom smiled, nodding. "Yes, he is. He has his father's smarts and his mother's charms."

"You look beautiful, Mom." I bent down and kissed her cheek.

"And you are handsome as ever." She took a step back and noticed Emily's hand linked with mine.

My mom brought her gaze back to mine and drew a breath. "Doesn't tonight just feel enchanting? Much better than Portugal?"

My dad frowned. "What's wrong with Portugal? We were having a lovely time."

I chuckled.

"Tonight is beautiful," Emily said, looking around the room. "I'm in complete awe over your florals and just… everything."

"We've got good people who know how to throw a party. Maybe if either one of my children ever decided to take dating seriously, I'd be able to throw them a wedding of a lifetime."

A blush touched Emily's cheeks, and she nodded. "You never know."

My mom groaned and shook her head. "No, I've got a pretty good idea that I won't be a grandma until I'm too old to remember that I am one. I mean, he had to drag his best friend to a gala. Your grandmother would not find this *poetic* at all, and she was into that stuff. You knew that, right?"

Surprise darted through me, and I shook my head. "I had no idea Grandma was into poetry."

"Well, she wrote. Didn't you ever read one of her books? They're in the library at the orchard." She raised her shoulders. "Anyway, she'd be very distressed that her grandchildren were anti-love when she wrote about it so beautifully."

Emily's eyes widened, and she glanced at me with a timid smile. I'd never seen Emily look sheepish, but I certainly detected that now.

"Actually, Mom, Emily and I—"

My mom clapped her hands and looked over my shoulder, completely unaware that she'd interrupted me. "Would you look who's here?"

"Who?" I could only guess my sister had decided to show up.

I turned around slowly, but when my eyes landed on the couple my mom spoke about, I froze before turning back around.

My mom waved them over as my jaw clenched.

"What are they doing here?" I asked in a low voice.

"Oh, your father ran into them at the store the other day. It's been eons, hasn't it?" My mom's eyes stayed on mine, and I knew what was about to roll off her lips. I held Emily's hand tighter before it hit.

"You know, Clara is back in town. She's divorced."

Emily's hand turned limp in my hand as my mom

kept muttering useless facts and figures about Clara's current life in Seattle.

I let go of her hand but offered her my arm, which she took without looking in my direction.

Clara's parents managed to arrive as my father greeted them both, and I just prayed Clara wasn't about to show up next.

Clara's mom eyed Emily with as much tact as expected before bringing her gaze to me.

"It's been too long," her mom said, smiling.

Not long enough.

"Indeed," I said, nodding. "Everyone, I'd like you to meet Emily, my girlfriend."

Clara's mom traded a look with my own, and I realized this had been a setup, of sorts, to warm me up to the idea.

"Girlfriend?" my mom asked, touching her chest. "Since when?"

"I've been begging her for a year, but it's only been recently that she's accepted the role," I teased, and Emily looked like she wanted to stab one of her heels into the top of my foot.

My mom cupped Emily's face with her palms and nearly squealed, which wasn't the reaction I'd expected.

"What are you going to tell all those women beating down your door?" my mom asked, suddenly looking askance at Clara's mom.

Emily's brows rose in amusement as she folded her arms over her chest. "Yes, do tell."

I could feel Clara's parents' eyes on us as I kept Emily's arm linked through mine.

"I haven't had to deal with that for quite some time," I explained.

Emily tilted her chin in my direction and cocked a brow. "How so?"

James and Amelia walked up to the group with their drinks when my mom tapped Amelia's arm. "They're an item."

"Indeed, they are." James laughed.

"You knew and didn't tell me?" my mom asked James indignantly.

"My son was just about to enlighten us about why he hasn't had to deal with fending off women," my dad explained.

"It's never quite been like that," I said, laughing.

"Oh, it's been pretty close," James said, chuckling as he took a sip of his martini. "But should I tell them or should you?"

Emily straightened. "Tell us what?"

"I haven't been on a date in months." My eyes stayed on Emily's.

"Of course you have. You were on one a few weeks ago. You said something about her being a messy eater and having to run around all night after her."

Clara's parents gasped.

James laughed. "And you'd still stand here with him after he told you that?"

Emily giggled. "He has a good heart."

My gaze locked on Emily's. "I couldn't even tell you when I've last been on a date."

"I could." Emily's brows rose in satisfaction, and I wondered if maybe she'd felt something for me longer than she'd cared to admit to herself or me.

"All of this man's dates…" James started as Amelia's smile widened.

"I can't believe you're going to let out my secret," I joked.

"James hasn't been a serial dater for quite some time."

Emily scowled. "Then, what have you been up to?"

"He's been babysitting Henry," Amelia said, chuckling, "so we could have date nights."

Emily drew in a shocked gasp, while my mom's smile widened.

"My son has finally grown up." My dad shook his head, patting my shoulder. "It's about damn time."

Emily looked as stunned as the rest of them while my mom moved toward Clara's parents and began talking in a low voice.

Obviously, whatever plan they had was about to be obliterated. A sigh of relief left my lungs as I realized that things were about to be okay.

Nina bounded up to us and draped her arms over my cousin. "What did I miss?"

I looked around her and frowned. "Where's your date?"

"Date? Why would I bring a date to Mom and Dad's anniversary?"

I scowled and scratched my head. "You told me we had to bring a date so we could dance with them."

She laughed. "You're so gullible. I just hoped that would be the final push to get you to bring Emily."

Emily burst into laugher, and I knew tonight couldn't get any better.

Chapter Nineteen

Emily

Dancing the night away with Lucas was like a dream. And the moment he'd said we were together made my worries disappear.

And it wasn't just because of the words. It was the expression in his gaze. I smiled, sitting back in my bed with my feet extended in front of me, pillows piled high behind me, and the comforter over my feet while I opened my laptop.

The afternoon sun filtered through the sheer drapes in my bedroom as I opened my inbox. The last few days at the store had been a whirlwind. Tourist season had hit, and it felt like with it came a monsoon of nonstop selling, shipping items back to their homes, and putting out new inventory.

I was exhausted. My house was a mess, and my grandparents were getting antsy because the physical therapist who came to the house three times a week felt that Mimi was ready to go back home.

Except for the slight issue of the stairs.

Which was the entire reason she was here, but all it took was for Mimi to hear a professional say she would be fine at her own house.

And of course, she'd be fine in her own house, but how do we get her there?

I chuckled at the thought, but dread filled me because I knew we wouldn't hear the end of it until we figured out a solution.

I sighed as my email populated and started scanning and deleting until I came to one that sent a jolt through me.

There was no way.

My eyes scanned the subject ten times before I opened it.

Could this be real?

Was it a trick?

I squinted my eyes as if that would make it

clearer, or less real, or just… anything but what it said.

Congratulations! You've been accepted as part of an elite group of poets and industry leaders to join the Great Smoky Mountain Poetic Residency.

"They liked my poems," I whispered, staring at my screen and afraid to actually open the message.

What if the rest of the message read, *you've been accepted to join in via zoom to see the real winners*?

No, this really was happening.

I sat in stunned silence as my mind whirred nonstop. My words meant something to someone.

My fingers zipped with excitement as I clicked the message open. My heart raced as my eyes scanned the specifics.

Three months' accommodations at the Great Smoky Mountain Retreat include food and beverages.

One-thousand-dollar monthly stipend.

Weekly workshop at the Artist House.

Bi-weekly lectures at the College of Poetics.

Monthly readings at Smoky Mountain Bookshop.

Chapbook published at the end of residency to include 500 personal and promotional copies.

I drew a shaky breath and let it out slowly. A thousand bucks wouldn't cover my house payment here, but I could pull from my savings.

And the thought of giving lectures terrified me. What did I know that they didn't?

I reread the letter and closed my eyes.

From the moment I saw this residency, it felt like it had spoken to me. After all, Grandma Cecilia loved the Great Smoky Mountains. It had felt like a sign from her.

Yet this was no longer following a whim or trusting my gut.

I actually got accepted and would have to uproot my life for three months, all to write poetry in peace and experience camaraderie with other poets.

But was I really a poet?

I suddenly felt like an imposter pretending to know what I was doing with words. I wasn't soulful or imaginative.

These words just plopped together and meant

something to me.

I let out a little groan and fell back on my pillows as I stared at the bottom of the message. I had one week to accept the offer before it was offered to another *poet*.

It was as if the world faded away, and apprehension filled my veins. My breath caught in my throat.

Lucas.

We'd finally made it over the hurdle. We were a couple. Would it be fair to expect him to do long-distance with me for a few months?

I shook my head at the thought. Was I just dooming our relationship from the beginning if I accepted this residency?

I closed my laptop and wandered out of my bedroom in a daze.

This morning, everything felt so easy and simple.

Like I was on the right track and then—*bam*.

"What's got you down?" Mimi asked, pushing her walker into the kitchen.

"Oh, nothing."

Mimi stopped in front of the fridge and opened

it, staring inside.

"Something I can help you find?"

"I thought there was some string cheese in here." She frowned.

"I'll find it." I made my way over and spotted it in the door. "Grandpa must have eaten it last."

"He never puts things where they belong," Mimi grumbled, and I laughed.

"And yet, here you are with him, all these years later."

Mimi chuckled and rolled away toward the table with the cheese in her hand.

"Okay, honey. Am I going to have to pry it out of you, or will you just tell your Mimi what's wrong?"

I smiled at her and grabbed an iced tea from the fridge. "If I accept, I'll be the new poet in residency somewhere in the heart of the Great Smoky Mountains."

Her eyes sparkled with excitement, and a little chuckle rang into the room. "Hot Dog! I knew you were good. When did you submit? How come you didn't tell anyone?"

I took a sip of tea and raised my shoulders. "In

case I didn't get it. I just didn't want anyone to know."

She frowned. "You don't want other people to be excited about your accomplishments?"

"If I didn't get in, it wouldn't be an accomplishment."

"Of course it would. You were brave enough to submit, and honestly, if they didn't choose your poetry, that's not because you're not good enough. It's because they have questionable taste."

"I love you, Mimi."

"So, then, what's the problem?" Her eyes stayed on mine as she opened up her cheese and took a seat.

"Well, I'd be gone for three months."

"Wow. Three months." She nodded. "That's a fair chunk of time."

"And I've just started dating Lucas…" My voice trailed off.

"So?" Mimi's brows knitted together. "What's the problem?"

I couldn't believe I was talking to Mimi about this, but there was something about her reaction that compelled me to keep going.

"Well, you know…"

Her brows quirked up. "I don't know."

"He's dated a lot of women, and we just started a relationship. What if this causes things to go south?"

"Darling, if three months apart is too much for him to handle, he's not worth your time." She let out a deep breath. "But if it means anything to you, I don't see that as being a problem. You can see it in his eyes."

"See what?"

"Complete and utter devotion."

"You think so?" I asked.

Mimi beckoned me over with a gentle wave of her hand. "You deserve this and everything the world has to offer."

I sat next to Mimi and let out a deep breath. "I'm just scared."

"Did you know that sometimes, your heart attracts the very things that scare you?" She tilted her head, studying me. "It's what helps us to grow and push ourselves. Make no mistake that having both of these opportunities crash into your life at the same time means something."

I nodded, quietly sitting next to her. She reached for my hands and brought them to her lap. The frail fingers, worn from eighty years in this world, clutched my hand in hers. The room grew still as she continued to keep her gaze on me.

"You do understand that you deserve these things." She narrowed her eyes on me. "Right?"

A lump unexpectedly formed in the back of my throat. "I don't know what I deserve, Mimi. I've been pretty happy here on Marigold. I love my little house, my job at the store, my family…"

"But what if your heart has room for even more?" she asked, and I realized Mimi had a way of soothing away troubles.

Tears brimmed my eyelids as I cleared my throat. "I do love Lucas."

She held my hands tighter. "I know you do."

"And I love the feelings my words bring me."

"You can't hide those from the words, Emily. You have a gift, just like Grandma Cecilia. She loved poetry."

My heart tugged for her, but I knew how lucky I

was to have Mimi in front of me too.

"I'm sure this sounds crazy, but the only reason I applied for this residency was because Grandma Cecilia loved the Great Smoky Mountains, and I truly never believed I'd be chosen."

"I believe it."

"Did you know that your grandmother and Lucas's grandmother were friends when they were younger?"

"Really?"

"Indeed." She nodded. "But their friendship fell apart."

"Why's that?"

"Mrs. Edwards was a poet, but so was your grandmother. The difference was that Mrs. Edwards shared the words with the world, but Grandma Cecilia was too afraid to do so."

I frowned, thinking about my other grandma. She never seemed like she was afraid of much.

"Cecilia was afraid of failure. So much so that she didn't even dare to try. When Mrs. Edwards submitted her poems and became a published poet, I hate to say it, but I think Cecilia became jealous." She drew in a breath. "My point in telling you isn't to cast a shadow over your grandma's memory but to make you realize that you should never let the fear of the unknown stop you from doing what your heart demands."

"I had no idea they were friends."

Mimi chuckled. "I have a long memory, but yes, they were indeed friends in their twenties, but it fizzled out. And I'm pretty certain that's why."

Mimi's words felt like a guiding light in a very uncertain moment.

After all, none of this would have been possible had I not submitted some poetry merely on a whim.

"So, I think you know the next step," Mimi continued.

"Accept the residency?"

She chuckled. "Well, yes… that. But also, tell Lucas the good news."

I smiled at the thought of sharing something so special with him. I was also grateful I'd mentioned it to him so that it wasn't a complete surprise.

Although, I think it would still shock him like it

did me.

"I think that's my cue to tell Lucas the news."

She tapped my hand before letting go. "I think so too."

Mimi winked at me and nodded. "Good things are on the horizon for you. I can feel it."

I drew a deep breath and let it out slowly. "Thanks, Mimi. I think I do too."

Standing from the chair, I pulled my phone out of my pocket and texted Lucas.

Hey, I have some interesting news to share. You at the orchard?

He immediately responded.

Just got back after dropping off the demon cat... I mean Oscar.

I chuckled and texted back.

Don't let Brad off the hook. He owes your family

a Ficus.

He can make it a wedding gift, and we'll call it even.

My heart skipped a beat when I reread the text.

"That look can't be replicated," Mimi said. "It's pure."

I flashed my eyes to hers, and I nodded. "It feels pretty special."

I wrote back a quick text.

I'll be there in a few.

I gave Mimi a kiss and made my way outside. The temperature had warmed up slightly, and it felt like summer was nipping at my fingertips.

The thought punched me in the gut.

I wouldn't be on Marigold Island for the summer. I'd be in the Great Smoky Mountains.

As I pulled on my pink helmet, I took a deep

breath, inhaling the sweet smell of the island's sea breeze and flowers that permeated my row of houses.

Things would be okay.

Pulling out of my driveway, I rode down the street toward the orchard. It was a magical place, and it was weird to think I'd be somewhere else for the next few months. Hopefully, I'd be back in time for their fall festival.

A knot formed in my stomach, and I let out a groan that melded with the crashing waves along the side of the winding road.

When I pulled up to the orchard, the gate was wide open, and I drove up and parked.

Lucas opened the door and smiled. "I've been counting the minutes."

I unfastened my helmet and made my way toward my boyfriend.

I liked how that sounded.

"Oh, yeah?"

Lucas nodded and walked down the steps, opening his arms as I dove in.

"You always make me feel safe," I whispered,

breathing in the intoxicating mix of his cologne and something unique to Lucas. It was just fresh and relaxing.

He brushed his lips across the top of my head, and my body tingled with need, but I knew I needed to tell him my news or I'd talk myself out of it, and I owed this to myself.

And Grandma Cecilia and Mimi.

I took a step back and fastened my gaze on Lucas. "We need to talk."

Chapter Twenty

Lucas

Emily's dark hair was nested in a pile on top of her head. Excitement mixed with something I couldn't quite gauge darted through her expression.

She linked her hands with mine, and we walked inside.

"My parents can't stop talking about you," I told her, and her smile only widened.

"I think their son is pretty spectacular too."

"Ah, shucks." I chuckled, not letting go of her hands as I drew her into me. I tipped my head down and caught her gaze. "Now, tell me what's on your mind. It's not Clara, is it? I had no idea my parents invited them, and my mom was so mortified when she realized you and I are together."

She smiled and chuckled. "Oh, please. She's old news."

I laughed, pulling her in tighter. I just loved how her body fit into mine. She lifted her head and traced my chest with her fingers.

"Remember that poetry contest?"

I nodded. "Yeah. I remember it. You didn't want to tell anyone about it."

She licked her bottom lip and drew a deep breath, but I kept hold of her.

"I guess you could say..." She stopped herself and let out her breath. "I guess you could say that I won."

My brows rose. "You won? As in, they offered you the residency?"

It felt like all the dreams of our first summer together were crumbling into a million pieces.

She nodded. "Yeah. Three months."

Excitement shook through me when I saw the hopefulness in her gaze. This was what she wanted. I wasn't going to stand in the way.

I couldn't.

"I am so freaking proud of you, Emily Evans." I

hugged her tighter and felt her press her cheek against my chest. "So proud of you."

I took a step back and took her in. She looked incredible in her tight jeans and fitted red top, but there was a current of something else that made her even sexier.

A newfound confidence?

I wrapped my arms around her again and tamped down the disappointment and worry that wanted to destroy this moment.

This was amazing news.

And I wasn't about to let my personal desires take away her dreams.

Because sometimes, dreams changed.

But for the first time in a long time, I wasn't scrambling to figure out my next move.

My only move was to stay put for Emily.

"Do you think I should take it?" she asked.

"I wouldn't let you say no," I said softly. "Although, I'm not sure you'd listen to me, anyway."

She chuckled and nodded. "True."

A few minutes of silence sat between us as we

stood embracing.

"Your heart is beating fast," she said, looking up into my eyes.

I nodded. "I think it's the thought of losing you."

"You're not losing me."

"No, you're right. Wrong choice of words." I bit my lip and let go of her as she moved toward the hallway.

I followed her lead and sat next to her on the couch in the gathering room.

"I won't lie," she said, moving her hand over mine. "I'm scared to death about leaving you... us."

"Scared?" There were a lot of emotions I expected to hear, but fear wasn't one of them. "Why's that?"

"I'm worried you might... get bored." Her eyes stayed locked on mine.

My heart clenched when I looked into her gaze.

Darkness rose in my blood, wishing I hadn't been so cavalier over the years with women. Now, I had to pay for those choices because my history scared the one and only woman I'd ever loved.

My telling her I'd changed wasn't enough.

And I wasn't sure what was.

"I'll wait however long it takes to get you back to Marigold."

I thought about her grandpa's words, *she's a flight risk*, and clenched my jaw, feeling the selfish pull to keep her here.

I smiled, touching her mouth with my thumb, feeling the softness of the mouth I wanted to devour and feel pressed against my own.

"And if you don't come back home, I'll follow you wherever you go for as long as you'll have me."

Her expression softened as she touched my fingers still on her lips. "You mean that?"

"Every word." I smiled. "But not in a creepy stalker, Clara way."

She chuckled and nodded. "There's a part of me that doesn't want to do it, but I know if I don't, in ten years I'll wonder... what if?"

"The one thing I've learned after seeing my cousin battle certain things in his life is to never let your choices leave you saying those two words."

Emily nodded slowly and sucked in a deep

breath.

"So, you'll wait for me?"

"Absolutely." My voice lowered a notch as she climbed onto my lap. "Just don't go falling for one of those poets who always know what to say. They can be tricky."

A mischievous glint flicked through her gaze and a low rumble of a laugh escaped her lips right when her hand found my crotch.

"They couldn't offer me the same level of satisfaction as you." A sultry look floated through her gaze, and I couldn't help but press my lips to hers.

Everything I'd loved about Emily was on full display.

She let out a little moan of happiness as we kissed, and I cupped her butt on my lap so she didn't slide off the couch.

"I'm going to miss this," she said between kisses.

"Do they allow conjugal visits?" I teased.

She laughed. "It's not prison, just poetry camp."

I groaned and let my head fall back onto the cushions. "It's going to feel like a prison while you're away, but I wouldn't have it any other way."

"Don't be so dramatic," she teased, and I sat upright.

"My cousin told me the same thing a few weeks back."

Her brows rose as she caged me in with her arms. "Oh, yeah? What about?"

I smiled and tilted my head, taking in her beauty. The mischievous glint in her eyes, the perky smile, the kindness… tenderness…

"You," I said, smiling.

She chuckled, resting her forehead against mine, and I knew I'd treasure each and every moment like this until she left.

"What is the date you have to leave?" I asked.

Emily straightened on my lap and slid her phone out of her back pocket. She toppled next to me and dangled her legs over my lap.

"I'll pull up the email." She scanned her phone and waited a few seconds before handing it to me.

"You're leaving in three weeks?" My eyes widened. "Wow. I… didn't expect that."

"I know. I'm worried about telling my sisters, but I know they'll want me to go for it."

"I could always fill in for you at the store," I playfully offered, and she chuckled.

"You wish."

I scanned the email invitation and let out a deep sigh. "Three months is a long time. I hope you know I plan on visiting you."

"I hope so," she said softly.

"I'll come to each of your readings, if you want. You know, for moral support."

Her gaze brightened. "You would?"

"Totally. I mean, I'd rent a house down the road from you too, but I think that might defeat the purpose."

She laughed, tucking a piece of hair behind her ear. "Probably. I'm not exactly great at getting out of my comfort zone. I hope I can handle this."

"I have zero worries on that front. You'll probably be running the residency by the time you leave."

"Funny thing," she said softly. "I guess the current resident gets a say on whoever applies for the following program."

"You'll do a great job," I assured her.

"I just don't want to crush someone's dreams." She glanced toward the window.

Raindrops started coming down, bouncing off the patio and streaming down the glass.

Our fingers tangled with each other's as we watched the beautiful northwest scene unfold in front of us.

"I've heard their storms are beautiful," she said softly, looking over at me. "My grandma always spoke about them."

"I can't wait to experience them with you when I visit."

She nodded, a smile surfacing on her beautiful mouth.

"I don't want to lie to you, Emily. It's going to be so hard having you leave, but the hard part is missing you, nothing else."

Emily rested her head on my chest and let out a happy sigh. "I wish I hadn't waited so long to let my guard down with you."

I pressed my lips to her and let out a deep sigh. "I'm kicking myself for that too. I should have told you sooner."

"Speaking of, I can't believe you've let me think that you've been going on all these dates with women nonstop." She eyed me with a wicked grin. "That's sadistic."

"I dropped as many clues as I could think of. Do you really think I'd comment about how loudly a woman eats or how I couldn't have a deep conversation, or worse, have to chase after them?"

She chuckled. "I just thought it was code for something."

I brought her in close, but the heaviness in my heart had already started. I knew I would miss her even more than I could imagine.

Emily turned toward me. Her eyes searched mine, and I realized I saw the same trepidation mirrored in her gaze.

"I kind of feel like it's Murphy's Law. Like, of course, I finally find my soulmate, and then I suddenly disappear for a few months because of a once-in-a-lifetime opportunity."

Soulmate.

Hearing that word from her lips made my world spin, knowing I'd made the right decision to tell her how I felt.

Things would be okay. We'd get through this.

"On so many levels, I can't believe this is happening." A soft tremor threaded through her voice. "It's like the longer I sit with the news, the more worried I'm getting."

"Don't overthink it, Emily. You're right. It's a once-in-a-lifetime opportunity."

She looked at me and nodded. "But so is this."

I pulled her into a hug, feeling the steady beats of our hearts. "Now, we're both overthinking things. Three months is barely anything. You'll be so busy, I doubt you'll even remember I exist."

She loosened her embrace and laughed. "Not likely."

"I mean, that's what I'm hoping happens."

Emily threw a soft punch in my direction and laughed.

I realized how it came out and chuckled. "I meant for you."

"Sure you did, buddy," she teased.

"You're about to embark on an incredible journey, and I will be there as much as I can without stepping on your toes," I promised. "And I won't get my feelings hurt if you tell me to buzz off."

"I would never do such a thing." She grinned. "Hey, how did Brad respond when you dropped off Oscar?"

I laughed. "Actually, I think he was surprised that I didn't buckle and ship him off somewhere else."

"Yeah?" She looked surprised.

"And he had a little heart-to-heart with me."

"No…" Her eyes widened.

"Yeah. You've got a good brother."

"I do." She nodded. "I've got a good family. A good boyfriend. An opportunity that I can't pass up." She turned to me, still holding her phone. "Should I hit *Accept*?"

I smiled. "If you don't, I will."

"Ah, trying to get rid of me so soon," she joked,

scrolling on her phone.

But before she had a chance to click *Accept*, I scooped her into my arms and kissed her harder than I ever had before, knowing things might never be the same.

Chapter Twenty-One

Emily

The weeks between accepting the invitation and today zipped by so fast that I still couldn't fathom that I was actually leaving today.

But as I stood at the airport with my entire family staring at me and my boyfriend, holding my hand tighter than usual, I knew there was no turning back.

Today was the day that I'd be listening to my heart again, but this time, I didn't know where it would lead or why I needed to listen.

My mom smoothed her hand over my hair and smiled, tears brimming her lids. "I know it's crazy and it's only three months and you're a grown woman…" She sniffled. "But I'm going to miss your glowing face at the store."

I chuckled, pushing down the lump in my throat. "You're just missing the cheap labor."

My mom chuckled and leaned in to plant a kiss on my cheek, followed by my dad and all my siblings. They all traded glances, gave me one last goodbye, and left Lucas and me alone to say our own farewell.

"I'm going to miss you so much, Emily." Lucas's gaze locked on mine. I saw the familiar intensity capture my heart as he stepped closer, cupping my face with his hands. His eyes fell to my lips before tearing his gaze away. He dropped his arms and glanced out the window to the terminal parking. "This is hard."

"It's not like it's our last kiss together," I said, feeling my chest tighten. Was he having a change of heart? Did he want to break things off to make it easier?

"What's wrong?" he asked tenderly, his thumb gliding along my jaw.

"Just crazy thoughts."

"Let me in. Tell me about those crazy thoughts."

I bit my bottom lip and took a deep breath. "Do you want to break things off until I get back?"

Pain darted through his eyes as his gaze

darkened. "Why would you ask that?"

"I just…" My voice broke off. "If something happens, I don't…"

"The only woman I want is you, Emily. Don't let your fears misguide you, but I promise you that I'll be honest with you. Always."

I nodded.

"You're woven into me. I can't escape you, Emily." His words swallowed me whole as his hand cradled my cheek. "I won't let you down. Our future is too important."

"I love you, Lucas."

His eyes stayed locked on mine. "I love you too, Emily Evans. Remember, this isn't just for you. This is for us. Because I don't ever want you to regret a moment with me."

I gasped at the beauty of his words. "You're the poet, Lucas."

He shook his head and brought his lips down to mine.

It was as if the rest of the bustling terminal drifted away into nothingness.

His warm breath skated across my lips, and I knew that every single day away from this man was going to be excruciating, but he was right.

Mimi was right. I needed to do this.

I took a step back, feeling the tingle on my lips as I shook my head. "I'm going to miss you like crazy, Lucas."

He nodded. "I know. It's time to go."

I grinned, pulling my carry-on. "It is."

"And remember, I'll fly anything you need out there."

I chuckled. "Maybe that's why I'm only taking a carry-on, so you have to fly out multiple times to bring me stuff."

Lucas laughed, and I tried to record the sound into my memory as he stuffed his hands into his pockets and kind of leaned sideways with a grimace.

"I love you, Emily. Go show them how poetry is written. Let 'em have it, and don't let any of those ivory tower people make you doubt yourself." He licked his bottom lip, and I pulled him in again for another kiss, feeling his tongue stroke mine with a raw need that we both craved.

I forced myself to stop kissing him and smiled. "Love you. I'll text you when I land."

Lucas nodded and turned around, walking toward my family.

If he hadn't, we'd still be standing there, not letting go.

I gave a last wave to my family and started toward the security checkpoint with my ticket and license out.

By the time I got to my gate, the flight was already boarding, which was good because I couldn't talk myself out of getting on the plane.

And every cell in my body was instructing me to turn around and run.

But I couldn't let fear guide me.

Mimi's words floated through my head, and I knew I needed to do this for both of my grandmas.

As I walked my way down the skybridge to the plane, my pulse raced with uncertainty.

Who did I think I was, going to Tennessee to study poetry? To teach poetry?

I quickly found my seat, shoved my suitcase in the bin, and slumped down in the seat, suddenly doubting everything about me and my poetry. The passenger sitting next to me buckled in and took out a laptop as I stared at my phone and the first line of the poem that got me here.

Sometimes, my heart has to scream until I finally hear the whispers, and that whisper led me to you.

I slid the tray down and set my phone down as I stared out the window.

A knot formed in my belly. I already missed my family.

Lucas.

My house.

I even missed Oscar.

Lucas was headed back to the island to babysit Henry tonight while Amelia and James stayed in the city for a date night.

I was already missing out on so much life, a life I loved.

Swallowing down a lump in my throat, I forced the tears away right when the woman sitting next to me cleared her throat.

"I'm sorry. I know I just violated every single social and airline etiquette scenario out there, but I saw that line on your phone, and it's beautiful."

Embarrassment flashed through me as my eyes connected with hers. "Thank you."

"Did you write it?" she asked.

I nodded, staring down at the sentence.

"Interesting." She smiled and nodded.

"I'm actually headed to Tennessee for a poetry residency."

Her lips curled up slightly. "Is that so?"

I drew in a deep breath. "For three months."

"That's quite a commitment."

"It is, but we only have one shot on this earth, and it goes by so quickly as it is." I bit my lip and thought about Grandma Cecilia. "I'm doing it for my grandmother. She was a poet, but she let fear keep her from her passion."

The lady's head tipped slightly. "Fear?"

"Fear of rejection."

"That's the worst kind, isn't it." She wasn't really asking.

The captain announced our departure, and I slipped my phone onto my lap.

"I should confess something to you," the woman confided.

"What's that?" I asked, unsure of what kind of confession needed to be traded between two strangers.

"I'm a literary agent." Her eyes twinkled. "And I'm intrigued."

"Wow. Thank you."

"No, thank you." She slid me a business card. "I'd love to see more of your writing."

"You would?" I asked, feeling my throat constrict for absolutely no reason.

"I would." She nodded. "Have you ever thought about writing a story about your grandmother?"

"I—" My mouth snapped shut while I thought about. A tale deserved to be told about her, no doubt. "I don't know if I'm skilled enough to do that."

"Doubt is such a powerful notion." She eyed me.

"Only those who truly believe in themselves are rewarded, while the rest of us are resigned to just imagine."

I smiled, acknowledging the irony. "Yeah. I have thought about writing about my grandmother. Should I send my proposal to your email on the card?"

I glanced down to see her name.

Cecilia.

I gasped. "Cecilia is my grandmother's name."

"It's a good name," she said softly.

I nodded. "It absolutely is."

By the time we got to cruising altitude, I knew that for the first time in my life, I'd silenced the beast of doubt and insecurity.

We didn't speak any more on the flight, but the moment the plane touched down, I no longer felt scared. I felt invigorated.

For the moment, I belonged here, and I wasn't going to fight it any longer.

I breathed out a breath of resilience for my grandma, for my family, and for Lucas. But mostly, for me.

And for the first time in a long time, I didn't feel like running.

"Emily Evans." A woman waved at me, holding a sign with my name.

I immediately recognized her.

Nadia.

She was the director of the program and had planned on driving me out to the cabin I'd be staying at and showing me around the small mountain town.

"So good to see you," Nadia said, looking behind me at my carry-on bag. "Is that all you brought?"

I laughed and nodded. "I'm a light packer."

"You'd have to be."

"Okay, right this way. It's a little over an hour to where you'll be staying. Everyone is so excited to meet you. Your words have touched a lot of people, and they can't wait to pick your mind and hear all about your process."

"My process?" I hadn't meant to say that aloud. "Oh, it's a pretty simple one."

"You're just being humble."

I suddenly craved to be back on the plane with

Cecilia where I didn't have to impress anyone. It had never occurred to me that these people would expect something more of me than I had to give.

I had no process.

I just…

Sat down and wrote.

But I was here now, and I'd better come up with something.

As we made our way to her car, I thought about what the next few months would look like. I glanced at Nadia and hoped she couldn't see right through me.

That I was an imposter dressed in a poet's cloak.

I buckled as she turned on the car, and I looked out the window.

She spoke of the cabin, her coworkers, students, and the little bookstore where I'd be giving readings, and all the while, my mind swirled with thoughts I couldn't contain.

But as we drove along the winding road, the mountains began to rise into a beauty I wasn't ready for.

Even though the sun was already beginning to set, the vision in front of me was surreal as the majestic mountains imposed their glory upon the landscape.

The clouds looked like ruffled feathers dusting the peaks of the glorious mountaintops.

"You should roll down the window. It smells incredible out here," she said, turning toward me.

"Yeah?"

She nodded as I did just that. A crisp sweetness teased my senses as I let my hands slide into the blowing air.

I closed my eyes and took it in, smelling the aromas of the Great Smoky Mountains, and I knew precisely why Grandma Cecilia loved this place.

I blinked my eyes open so I wouldn't miss a second more.

An awareness of humility scraped over me as I dared to trespass on nature's most beautiful poem of all. The massive vastness of land stretched before me with peaks and valleys struggling to capture nature's beautiful hues that clashed with the awareness of what lay ahead of me. The rolling hills and mysterious valleys beckoned my imagination, and I knew without a shadow of a doubt that this was where I belonged.

"And here we are," she said, glancing at me.

It hadn't even felt like fifteen minutes, let alone an hour.

"Already?"

She smiled and nodded. "Just down this drive."

As we drove up to the cabin, my heart pounded in my chest. The woods along the drive sheltered the cabin and tucked it away from the world. She turned off the car, and I stepped outside.

The profound silence swept through me, leaving an intense amount of serenity that I didn't even realize I'd been craving.

Nadia shut her door and glanced over at me. "Beautiful, isn't it?"

I smiled and nodded. "It's magical."

She pointed at me and grinned. "See? Right there. That's what we want to capture from you."

I shook my head, unsure of what she meant.

"You see the mysticism where others don't." She nodded. "But you're right. This place is magical."

I drew a deep breath, feeling the fresh air flow deep into my lungs, and I knew this was where I belonged.

Chapter Twenty-Two

Lucas

It was hard not to think about the words her grandfather told me—*she's a flight risk.*

Well, she'd already forgotten to text me when she landed, and I suddenly started feeling like I was losing Emily before I'd truly had her.

But there would be nothing worse than losing her to regret, and I certainly didn't want her to regret dating me and missing out on something to do for her personal growth.

I let out a deep breath and stared at the text I'd sent this morning.

Miss ya already. I've even started borrowing Oscar to cuddle with. Have fun!

I hadn't heard back yet, and I'd sent it a couple of hours ago. But I knew she'd probably been swamped since she'd arrived. Someone from the program was going to pick her up last night, show her the place she'd be staying, and take her to town for dinner.

She probably crashed in bed before she had a chance to send a text.

But I had heard through James that she'd texted Amelia last night, so I at least knew she was safe. That was my initial concern when I'd been met with silence.

I swallowed my own doubts and walked over to the foreman standing in front of the apartment complex we were rehabbing.

At least with Emily in Tennessee, I'd be able to throw myself into this nightmare of a project because there was no doubt this building needed me.

The previous owners of this complex were haphazard at best.

"You think we'll get Building A complete by midsummer?" I asked.

My foreman, Todd, pushed his mouth into a

frown. "As long we can get the contractors to show up. That's been half the battle."

I nodded in agreement just as my phone buzzed. Hoping it was Emily, I pulled it out only to be let down.

It was James. He could wait.

Joe, the assistant project manager, walked over, staring at my foreman with a displeased look.

There was tension in the air, and it wasn't even eleven in the morning. I usually liked the organized chaos at building projects, but this one had been the pits from the start. I pulled my hard hat down tighter as Joe cleared his throat.

"Plumber just pushed us out until Tuesday." He gritted his teeth and shook his head. "We can't just use this guy because he's your wife's cousin."

My gaze flew to Tood. "The plumber is your wife's cousin."

"Yup, but his bid came in lower."

I shook my head. "Doesn't matter much if he doesn't show up."

Joe nodded. "Ditto."

"I'll call him and see what's going on," Todd

grumbled, walking away.

"I had no idea Todd hired a relative."

Joe shrugged and looked toward the building in question.

"What do you think?"

"About what?"

"Think we can get it done before fall?"

"Not if we keep hiring Todd's relatives."

I chuckled and nodded in agreement as I walked toward the building and the maze of materials and equipment that were sitting in the parking lot.

When I reached the apartment building, I looked up and scanned the structure. At least it would be a solid investment when it was all over with.

My phone buzzed, and I pulled it out to see a text from Emily. My entire body relaxed the moment I realized the message was from her.

Apparently, I hadn't done a great job of pretending to myself that I wasn't concerned that she hadn't texted last night or this morning.

That is very desperate and very questionable.

Sorry I didn't text. I messaged my sister last night, crawled in bed to text you, and woke up this morning to Nadia honking her horn outside the cabin. Place is great. Magical, really. I didn't know I'd be able to find a place as amazing as Marigold. Off to workshop some of my writing. Love you.

I chuckled at her response about Oscar and wrote a quick love you back and felt great about her excuse for not texting last night or this morning.

But I couldn't get my mind to skip over her love for her new surroundings. The kicker was that if her grandpa hadn't wandered outside that one morning, I never would have thought about it. Now, the idea of her running away and never coming back was on the top of every thought.

My phone rang with a number I didn't recognize, and I let it go to voicemail as I watched Todd make his way back over.

"Plumber issue is resolved."

"Yeah?" I asked. "He's coming when originally scheduled?"

Todd shook his head. "No. I fired him, but the

new plumber will be here tomorrow."

I chuckled. "Ouch. That's going to make for a rough holiday dinner."

Todd smiled and let out a deep breath. "Honestly, it was a favor for my wife. His bid came in low, so I gave him a chance."

I nodded, feeling the buzz of the voicemail notification in my pocket. "It sounds like we're back on track, and the drywallers will be able to come when they're scheduled next? No relative situation with them, I hope?"

Joe chuckled as Todd shook his head, and I made my way to my truck.

When I slid inside, I pulled out my phone and clicked on the voicemail, thinking it was probably just spam.

And then I heard it.

Clara left a message, hoping to catch up over coffee.

I stared out my windshield, wondering what world I was in where the woman I wanted was thousands of miles away, and the one I couldn't run from fast enough seemed to be within a one-mile radius at any given second.

Emily couldn't come home fast enough.

I checked my message from James, who happened to be in Seattle today and wanted to do lunch around noon. I shot him a quick message telling him that sounded great with the name of the place to meet.

I pulled out of the parking lot and thought about Emily already settling in. She always had been a bit of a free spirit, so it wasn't like I didn't expect her to go with the flow and enjoy her surroundings out there, but for her to compare the two and put it in the same league as Marigold Island meant something.

Three months wasn't long, but it was long enough to start missing family.

So, if I wasn't enough of a reason to come back, hopefully, they were.

A knot formed in my stomach at the thought, and I chuckled, realizing how badly I'd fallen for her.

As I navigated Seattle traffic, I found myself getting annoyed a little more and craving the simplicity of Marigold, where traffic only happened when the ferry pulled up.

I gripped the steering wheel a little tighter and groaned before turning on the radio to distract me.

But as some love song drifted over the speakers, all I could do was think about Emily.

I'd never been so excited to pull into the parking lot of a restaurant as I was today. I needed a distraction desperately, and it had only been day one.

What had happened to me? When I'd been friend-zoned by Emily, I could go weeks without seeing her, but now it was literally painful.

I spotted James's car, parked next to it, and went inside, spotting him in the corner booth.

He smiled and waved as the waitress brought over a cup of coffee for him. I took a seat and ordered the same. "This place has amazing patty melts."

James picked up the menu as the server brought over my coffee.

"How's Emily?" James asked, putting the menu down.

"I've only gotten one text from her, and she sounded pretty busy."

He nodded. "Yeah. That's what Amelia got from it too. How are you holding up on day one?"

"Totally fine. Don't even remember she's gone." I ran my fingers through my hair and groaned. "I'm a mess. Complete disaster. It's only three months, and I'm already terrified of losing her."

James chuckled and shook his head. "Being in love is rough."

"I just can't believe it." I twisted my lips into a contemplative pout. "And she seems to love it there. Even said it's as magical as Marigold."

James's brows rose in surprise. "Really? Emily said that?"

"So, that is worrisome, right? Coming from one of the Evans sisters?"

"Well, if Audrey said it I wouldn't even blink, but the other three? Yeah… I'd be concerned."

"I just hope the humidity hits hard, and she'll be begging to come home."

"Nice."

I chuckled. "You know what I mean."

"Well, she's in the hills, so it probably won't be

as bad there, humidity-wise."

I glared at my cousin. "You're not helping, man."

"When are you thinking of visiting her?"

I shrugged and took a sip of coffee as the server came over. "I don't want to seem pushy. I want her to have the full experience."

We both placed our orders and thanked the server.

"But you want her to feel needed," James pointed out.

"True. So, maybe sound a little needy?"

"No, you don't want to sound needy. You want her to feel needed. Dude, you are a mess."

"I know. It's like my instinct on how to navigate this relationship went out the window the moment it counts."

"Well, just maybe plan a time to go back there when you next talk to her."

"This probably sounds crazy, but I totally assumed we'd be talking multiple times a day. I mean, maybe for just a few minutes, but you know…"

James nodded. "Yeah, but she's only been there

a day."

"Okay. I have to confess something that's been eating at me the moment it happened."

James looked concerned. "Go on."

"Well, when I was waiting for Emily to come outside so I could drive her to work, her grandpa came to the car and tapped on the window."

"Okay." He lifted a brow and took another sip of coffee.

"And he said she was a flight risk."

My cousin's brows knitted together. "A flight risk? Like she's a runner?"

I nodded. "I didn't give it much credence because she loves Marigold Island, and why would she have reason to leave?"

"And then this." James nodded. "Well, now I understand why you're such a jumpy little fella now."

"Hardee-har-har." I sat back in the booth. "So, this wouldn't worry you?"

"I mean, I'd file it away, but I'd make sure she remembers how amazing you are."

I scratched my chin and grinned. "So, you think

I'm amazing?"

My cousin laughed as my phone rang. I glanced down to see Clara again.

"You're not going to believe this."

"What?" James asked, leaning over to see my phone.

"It's Clara. She's already left a message this morning about wanting to do coffee. I don't know how else to get the message across to her that it's not happening."

James nodded in agreement. "How about you invite her out now? I'm here. We're in public. I can surely help to get the point across."

"You think that's a good idea?"

"I think if we don't do something, she'll just keep bothering you.'

I nodded in agreement and picked up the phone, hoping I wasn't making a mistake.

Chapter Twenty-Three

Emily

To say I was exhausted was putting it mildly. It wasn't just about attending writing workshops, listening to lecturers, trying to come up with my own lecture to give, and then beginning to work on a project to present at the end of my stay… no, it was also that I was expected to socialize with these people.

And they were nice enough. We all had a common interest, which was a love for poetry, but trying to be on at all times was extremely tiring. And I depended on other people to give me a ride, for the most part.

But I was grateful every single morning that I woke up in this beautiful place.

"Okay, we've arrived at your destination," Ethan

said, glancing over at me.

I stared at the cabin, wondering how we'd already gotten from the café where we all workshopped for three hours to my cabin. I was definitely in a fog of exhaustion.

"So, should I pick you up tonight for dinner and drinks with the gang?" he asked.

My heart twisted into a tight knot at the thought of going out again.

Did I mention that everyone seemed to be ten years younger than me and not have a tired bone in their body?

Ethan included.

"I don't know, Ethan. I probably should carve out some time to work on my project."

"Oh, come on. I promise I'll get you home early."

My phone rang, and I absent-mindedly picked up. "Hello?"

"Did you get the flowers?"

"Flowers?" I asked, relishing the fact that I could hear a familiar voice.

"Yeah. I thought you said you'd be back at the

cabin by now."

"Oh, we just pulled up," I said, feeling my heart hammer in my chest.

I can't believe he sent flowers.

"Oh, I see them," Ethan told me, pointing at the porch.

"Who's that?" Lucas asked as I craned my neck to see a beautiful and natural looking bouquet.

"It's Ethan. He gave me a ride home. We just pulled into the driveway."

"Home."

"Well, you know what I mean..." I said, laughing.

I mouthed thanks for the ride to Ethan as I started out the door.

"Then should I count on picking you up for dinner?" Ethan asked.

I froze as the other end of the phone went silent.

"Are you going to answer him?" Lucas finally asked.

I sighed into the phone and looked at Ethan. "Yeah. That's fine. Just text me when."

"Will do, poet in residence."

I smiled and shut the door as I trudged to the porch of the cabin with Lucas not making a sound on the other end.

My stomach clenched with each step forward.

I knew how it looked, and the fact that I was here, and Lucas was there, and we had all this in between wasn't good.

I knelt down, and my heart melted when I realized what these flowers actually were.

"Oh, my gosh." I sucked in a breath. "Lucas, these are wildflowers. They're gorgeous."

"And probably illegal, but the florist didn't ask questions."

I picked them up and let myself into the cabin, which suddenly felt extremely isolating and cold.

I turned on the light and set the flowers on the kitchen counter, which opened up into the rest of the living space. A bedroom loft overlooked the small cabin. It was perfect for one person, or maybe half a person.

All I knew was that I had a very quiet Lucas on the other end of the phone.

"I'm putting you on speakerphone."

"No problem," he said flatly.

"Ethan is —"

"I didn't ask," he interrupted.

"But you want to."

"I don't know that I do."

I breathed in worry and closed my eyes. "He's a kid. They're all kids. I feel like some grandparent, teaching them the way of imagery."

"I didn't say a word."

"Exactly. You haven't said a word since you heard Ethan on the phone."

"I just wanted to make sure you got the flowers."

"They are gorgeous and so thoughtful." I sat on the couch and propped my head on the pillow. "I'm so lucky to have you."

"You mean that?"

"More than you know." I let out a deep breath. "But I'm absolutely exhausted. They never stop. And I'm still expected to give lectures, workshop poems, attend lectures, and then meet them for coffee, hang at lunch, go out for dinner."

"More than you bargained for?" Lucas's tone loosened up a bit.

"A lot, but did I tell you what happened to me on the plane?"

"This is our first real conversation since you got there," Lucas said softly, and I suddenly realized he was right.

I'd been here for eight days, and this was the first time I'd actually been able to talk with Lucas. Every other time, I was either at a reading, or busy scouring poems and crossing out lines.

I. Was. A. Horrible. Girlfriend.

"Lucas, I'm so sorry. This wasn't how I envisioned it."

He laughed and let out a deep breath. "Me neither. So, what happened on the plane?"

"I happened to be seated next to a literary agent, and she saw one of my poems."

"Yeah?"

"And she loved it. She gave me her card, and I've since emailed her some of my work and a proposal for a story about Grandma Cecilia."

"You're kidding."

"No. I'm not."

"And none of that would have happened if you hadn't accepted this residency." I could hear the smile in his voice, and it lifted me up and gave me the energy I needed. "I'm so proud of you, Emily."

I felt like I was floating on clouds. "I miss you."

"I miss you more."

"I doubt it."

"No, I'm pretty certain of it. Unlike you, I have painfully suffered through eight long days and nights without you. I have no hot, young stud named Ethan to take me out for dinner and drinks while shoving poetry in my face at breakfast."

I chuckled. "I just want you to know that neither of those things is happening consecutively."

"I believe you."

"I know you do." I laughed. "But just for context, I want you to close your eyes."

"Oooh, I like where this is going," he said, laughing.

"And picture a lanky guy who looks like he's still

a junior in high school with high tops, a shirt that hasn't been washed for weeks, if not longer, and greasy hair that he slicks back with his own spit. That, my love, is Ethan."

"You lost me at high tops," Lucas said, laughing. "And here I thought we were on to something."

I smiled at the thought and closed my eyes. "I'd be down, if you were."

"Oh, yeah." His voice lowered into the velvety goodness I loved and I let out a happy sigh.

"Then let's make a date. You, me, the phone, and ten o'clock my time."

"Wear something sexy," Lucas said.

"How about nothing at all?" I teased.

He groaned into the phone and let out a deep breath. "This is going to be a rough afternoon."

"Glad I could do my part to keep you interested," I teased.

"You don't have to work hard at that," he promised. "But I was wondering when I could come out there for a visit…" His voice trailed off.

"Did you still want to try to make it to a reading?"

"Absolutely."

"My first one is coming up in two weeks."

"That will be three weeks without you. This is torture." He cleared his throat. "But worth every second."

"I am learning a lot about technique and realizing how little I know."

"You know enough to be good. You have a voice that's unique enough to capture the attention of complete strangers. To me, that's plenty."

"You always know how to make me feel amazing."

"That's my job, babe."

I yawned into the phone on accident, and he let out a low laugh. "Do you have any classes or workshops this afternoon?"

"No. I finally have a few hours off." I groaned. "That is until Ethan comes back to pick me up for dinner."

"Maybe you should take a nap."

"Music to my ears. It would be the first batch of sleep since I got here. I'm still not quite used to sleeping in the middle of nowhere by myself. It's kind of unsettling."

"I wish I could be there with you."

"Me too," I said softly, and I meant it with every ounce of my being.

"Send me the dates of your readings, and I'll book my flights."

"Will do, and don't forget about our date tonight."

"Oh, you do not need to worry about that."

"I love you, Lucas. Thank you for the bouquet of wildflowers. They mean the world."

"You are my world, Emily." He sighed into the phone. "And I'm sorry about getting all worked up over nothing. It's just this long-distance thing plays havoc on me."

I chuckled. "A little jealousy never hurt anyone."

"I'll have to remember that."

"Love you, Lucas," I said softly while holding in a yawn.

"Love you too."

And with that, he hung up.

I let out a deep breath and stared at the planked ceiling, finally feeling like a bit of the whirlwind around me was slowing down.

When I'd first arrived here, things felt peaceful and enchanting. I felt like I could almost feel my grandma's spirit in the woods, but then I got hit with all the aspects of this residency that I'd underestimated.

I glanced at the calendar on my phone, and it gave me the willies. There were very few moments of inactivity, and that didn't count all the impromptu gatherings either. I scanned the dates for the readings and sent them over to Lucas.

Making my way to the front door, I opened it wide and felt the warm air skate across my skin as I stepped outside.

The birds chirped in the trees around the cabin. Squirrels hopped to their destinations, and I suddenly missed Chester and his family. I hoped my sisters were still feeding them.

My mind drifted to Marigold Island, and love swept over me as I wandered through the woods here, breathing in the fresh air and listening to the sounds that were so very different from my island. And what occurred to me was that not only did I love Marigold, but I loved the people there even more.

And I missed them greatly. I found a rock to perch myself on as I thought about what Mimi had said about Grandma Cecilia.

Was it true? Had she actually wanted to share her poetry with the public? The thought made me sad if she had wanted to do so but didn't have the courage. Or maybe it was the fault of our society, where we valued everyone's opinions to the point of dampening the creators' spirit?

Rejection was tough. People's opinions could be rough. But the truth was that for every person who wanted to say something negative, there were ten times as many who were supportive.

I'd always found that the people who felt the need to pick apart art or scream from the top of their lungs that they didn't like something were often lacking themselves. It was like the first and hopefully only one-star rating on Mae's little coffee shop.

The person complained that my sister only

offered coconut macaroons instead of chocolate-covered coconut macaroons. But my initial thought when I read the review was *hell*... At least my sister's waking up in the morning and making the macaroons. The same couldn't be said for the person leaving the review.

And honestly, seeing that review gave me the confidence I needed to come here because even if some people didn't like my poetry, maybe some others would. So what if I didn't dip my poems in chocolate? Go find someone who did.

That seed of rejection was also what stopped me from letting myself believe in Lucas and me. All this stuff was tied together into a perfect bow of imperfection that allowed me to understand that it was okay to find the people who appreciated me, and I was beyond grateful that Lucas was one of them.

I stretched toward the cloudless sky and yawned again, knowing I had to get some sleep or I might mention to Ethan that spit was not hair gel and then I'd be the person complaining about plain macaroons.

Chapter Twenty-Four

Lucas

The moment the driver let me off at Emily's cabin, my heart literally started racing. I couldn't believe I was finally here. We'd managed to schedule several phone dates, but all I wanted was to hold her in my arms, smell the sweetness of her hair, and hear her voice.

Emily swung open the green door to the cabin and held her arms up as I dashed over, tossed my bag on the ground, and picked her up, swinging her in my arms.

Her lips crashed to mine, and it felt like the weight of the world had finally lifted. Her lips tasted as sweet as I remembered, her smell was as intoxicating as last time, and hearing the little moan of her voice sent me over the edge.

We held each other for a long few minutes,

memorizing this moment and hoping it would get us through until next time.

I finally let Emily down, and she smiled wider. "You look extremely handsome."

"I shaved," I said, running my fingers over my face.

"Come on in," she said as I picked up my bag and followed her inside.

I glanced around and set my stuff down. "The tour you gave me on the phone certainly made this place look more spacious."

She laughed and nodded. "It's like a shoebox, but I am extremely grateful for the washer and dryer. There's no dishwasher, but it's just me."

I laughed. "I'd hope it's just you."

She giggled, and the sound made me crave her even more, but I knew we didn't have time for that.

Emily's reading was in an hour, and she'd told me Nadia would be picking us both up and heading down to the local bookshop any second. My flight landed late, so I was worried I wouldn't even get here in time.

"Are you nervous?"

"Kind of, but I realized the worst that happens is I stumble over my words." She grinned. "I mean, I've already come to realize that some people will pick apart my poetry for a good cause and then others… not so much."

I laughed. "You're braver than me."

"I doubt that."

"Did you want anything to drink?" she asked. "I have water, water, and more water."

"You know what? I'll take some water."

She chuckled and filled up a glass and brought it over to me as we both sat on the couch.

"I kind of feel bad," I confessed, turning to look at her.

"For what?"

I laughed. "I thought you had it better than you do."

"Thanks." She shook her head and let out a yawn. "The sleeping situation isn't getting any better. I know there are things in the woods at night. The problem is that I don't know what they are or if they respond to a name like Bob."

I took a sip of water. "Yeah, that's not exactly a great thing to think about."

"There are times when I think about just calling a rideshare and heading into a town to stay at a hotel for a night or two."

"What stops you?"

She stretched her legs in front of her as she slid onto the couch more. "I don't want to look like *that girl*." She used quotes and sighed. "I'm already older than most of the people I'm around. I don't want to be high-maintenance."

"I don't think wanting to feel safe is exactly high-maintenance."

"The thing is that I know I'm safe out here. It's just my imagination and the fact that I'd rather be someplace else."

My eyes locked on hers. "You would?"

She nodded. "But it's only seven more weeks."

I chuckled. "Yes, only seven."

The sound of a vehicle turning down the drive made Emily shoot from the couch. "Oh, my goodness. Okay, now my nerves are shot."

"How'd you go from as cool as a cucumber to completely destroyed in a matter of seconds?" I stood, pulling her into me. "You've got this."

"I don't got this." She shook her head and pushed on her temples. "I really don't got this."

"You do, and I'll be cheering for you every step of the way. Think back to Charles." I let go of her and walked over to my bag, pulling out a fedora just like the one he wore.

I put it on, and she chuckled. "Should I wear it, or should you?"

She smiled wider. "You won't believe this, but remember while we were there, and I told you I said, maybe you'll get lucky tonight, but I was talking about the hat?"

"Yeah, I remember. What about it?"

She blushed and looked so damn cute. "I thought you had said to me, 'You're so cute. If only I could make you gasp like that', not that you wanted a hat like that..."

I let her shift her weight a few times before chuckling.

"You want to know a little secret?"

"What?"

"That's what I said."

Emily burst into laugher and shook her head. "I can't believe you, Lucas Edwards. You'd let me squirm like that knowingly?"

I laughed, tugging the hat over her head and pulling her close. "I love seeing you squirm."

A horn honked twice, and I swept a quick kiss across Emily's lips as her laughter eased and she gave me the hat back.

"You should be ashamed of yourself," she teased, and I looped my fingers around hers as we made our way to Nadia's car.

She turned to me and gasped. "I forgot my poems. I'll be right back."

I watched Emily dash back up to the cabin as I climbed into the backseat of the car.

Nadia introduced herself and smiled at me through the rearview mirror. "It's nice to put a face with the man. She talks about you nonstop."

"Really?"

"Indeed." She grinned as Emily dashed our way

and got into the front seat.

"It's going to be a full house. The poetry readings are always a big deal in town."

"Oh, great." Emily laughed, putting her head against the neck rest.

"You've done readings before, right?" Nadia asked.

"No. Never."

"Oh, wow. Well, you'll do amazing. I'm sure with the beautiful night out, the crowd won't be so big."

I chuckled as Nadia smiled at me in the rearview mirror.

As she drove along the winding road, heading back into the town I'd only just driven through minutes ago, I could see why Emily fell for this place. It was majestic. The rolling hills, large peaks, and wide valleys created a picture unique to this region.

"There it is," Nadia said as we slowed down and drove by the bookstore.

It was standing room only, and I could feel the tension roil through Emily's body.

"How about I let you two out, and I'll go find a

place to park? It might be tricky tonight." She smiled at Emily. "But that's what happens when you're out making a name for yourself so much."

Emily laughed. "I didn't think I had a choice. Ethan and everyone else are pretty persistent."

"They are."

As she pulled to a stop, I saw a group of people make their way to the car as Emily opened the door. I got out behind her and noticed they were treating her like a celebrity.

Emily glanced at me and held out her hand for me to hold as the guy who could only be known as Ethan turned to face me.

"Hey, you must be Lucas." He gave me a quick handshake with my free hand and nodded. "She's a great gal. So fun. We're trying to convince her to stay longer."

"Oh, yeah?" I asked, glancing in Emily's direction.

"She seems pretty adamant about going back home, though," he said, shaking his head.

"Darn families," I said, laughing.

Emily squeezed my hand and pulled me closer as

she started introducing me to the students, faculty, and board members she'd been working with these last several weeks.

They all seemed to respect and admire her, which gave me comfort that she was in the right place.

As we made our way into the bookshop, the crowd swayed and shifted to let us through as the owner waved Emily over to where a minimal stage had been set up in the back of the shop. There was a lone microphone, a chair, and a small table with a cup of water on it.

Emily glanced at me, suddenly looking terrified.

"You've got this," I whispered.

"You think so?"

I nodded. "I know so. And if all else fails, we can always take a red-eye back to Seattle and pretend it never happened."

She chuckled and swiped the Fedora from my head, gently placing it on hers.

"Do I look more artsy?"

I laughed, nodding.

I took a seat that had miraculously been saved for me and watched her walk onto the small stage. Her vulnerability couldn't be missed as she laid out her papers and scanned the audience.

"Good evening, everyone," she said, breathing slowly. "It's an honor to be here tonight."

The audience clapped, and I followed their lead.

She waited until it died down and began reciting her poetry.

The room went silent, and a transformation happened between page and voice. She'd look up every so often, but the audience went still.

It felt as if everyone lived the poems through Emily's voice.

I closed my eyes and heard her words speaking directly to me.

The stories of our past scraping to tear up our futures

> *They will not define us*
> *But will be whispered to the void*
> *Where silence welcomes the unworthy*
> *But you are worthy*
> *Without history to judge us*

We will trust again…

Her voice was like a melody, putting me in an imaginative trance. The rise and fall of her breaths against the microphone. The cadence. The rhythm. The meaning.

I opened my eyes to see the woman who'd opened my eyes to the world and made me trust again.

Emily's dance with words was unlike anything I'd ever heard before. As her dark hair cascaded down her shoulders and her eyes lit up with the thrill of poetic storytelling, I knew that this was the woman I was meant to be with.

Now, I just needed to show her the sign.

Chapter Twenty-Five

Emily

As quickly as he came, he left. It felt like he took a piece of me with him, but I knew I needed all the time I had left here to work on my project. My hope was to turn in a very rough draft of poems to my agent that could be the basis of the story about Grandma Cecilia. I was already at the halfway point because instead of sleeping at night, I'd been listening to the sounds outside and trying to distract myself with writing poetry.

But I needed every second of time I had here because I was pretty certain that the moment I got back to Marigold, I'd become swept up in life back home, and I had to admit, I couldn't wait.

It had been two entire weeks since Lucas had left, and we'd still been texting nonstop, and we'd made sure to have our phone dates.

Those were always fun.

As I poured some cereal into a bowl, my phone buzzed.

Expecting it to be Lucas, I was surprised to see a number I didn't recognize. I opened it up and took a mouthful of cereal as I read the message.

I set the phone down and read it again, slurping on another spoonful of cereal.

I couldn't quite fathom what I was seeing.

While the cat is away, the mice will play.

I stared at the photo of Clara sitting at the orchard of Lucas's grandparents. She wasn't in the area they used for the public gatherings. She was sitting on the steps out back, overlooking the water.

Anger nipped inside me as I stared at her words and the smirk on her face.

But I didn't see Lucas. He was either smart enough not to be photographed or dumb enough to think she wouldn't document her visit.

Lucas wasn't dumb.

I forwarded the photo to him and slurped another spoonful of cereal into my mouth.

He answered instantly.

Why did you send me a pic of Clara?

I wrote back.

I'm trying to figure out why she sent me a picture of herself at your family's estate?

A minute or two passed by before I received another text.

I didn't even catch that she was there.

I chuckled to myself, feeling the knot in my stomach loosen a bit.

Well, I did.

He texted back.

You know how I feel about her.

I wrote back a raised shoulder emoji and then thought about what next to say.

I'm honestly a little worried and perplexed about why she's there. My parents are back in Portugal, and Nina is in New York, and James wouldn't have a reason in the world to let Clara hang out there.

I let out a sigh and shook my head.

You could have Brad run by the orchard and see if she's still there? It's kind of creepy. I don't know how she got my number, either.

He wrote back.

Well, I certainly didn't give it to her.

I pressed my lips together.

Maybe you should. She seems to struggle with boundaries.

He texted back a sideways emoji and a new text.

Thanks, Captain Obvious.

I switched over to Clara's text and found a not-so-poetic way of telling her to buzz off, and for the first time since finding out about her, I felt good.

I sucked on my bottom lip for a few seconds and forwarded the message I'd sent to Clara to Lucas. That would be the test of acceptance.

He immediately wrote back a smiley face.

You have a way with words. I bet the problem is solved.

I chuckled and wrote back that I loved him before

finishing up my cereal.

The familiar sound of Ethan's car idled out front, and I grabbed my folder to meet him outside.

I locked the door and bounded toward the car as he gave me a quick wave.

As I slid in the passenger seat, my phone buzzed again, but this time, there was a recent pic of Clara and Lucas. It was a selfie of her, and he was sitting next to her, seemingly unaware she was taking a photo. But that didn't matter. The point was that they were together.

My heart seized as I stared at the selfie. They were out in public somewhere, and she had a very coy expression on her face.

I spotted planters full of geraniums and overflowing petunias, so it had to be a recent shot.

Ethan started pulling out of the drive, but I put my hand up and coughed.

"You know what? I'm not feeling well." I glanced at him.

"You don't look so well either."

I nodded and clutched my folder. "I think I need the day off."

"Totally. I'll let the others know."

I thanked him and got out of the car as quickly as I could before I got sick.

By the time I went inside the cabin, my stomach had squeezed out all the cereal it could, and I moved slowly over to the couch and spread out.

It was just a picture, so I didn't know why my body was reacting this way.

But it was a picture with Lucas.

And he didn't mention anything.

Hadn't mentioned anything.

Wasn't that something you mentioned?

I turned on my side and closed my eyes.

Between the exhaustion, the photos, the confusion, and the jealousy rearing its ugly head, I needed to sleep desperately.

But I also needed to know what the heck was going on?

There was no way this photo could be real, yet here it was on my phone, sent by a woman who shouldn't even have my number.

I held my phone and brought in a deep breath,

trying to figure out what to say. No words would come.

For once in my life, I couldn't think of a thing to say. Tears unexpectedly filled my eyes as I turned on my back and stared at the wood-planked ceiling. The rustic ceiling fan dangled over me, putting me in a dizzy spell of regret.

The thing I needed most from Lucas was trust.

I clenched my eyes shut and felt the tears rolling down my cheeks.

This was ridiculous.

It had to be a lack of sleep toying with my mind.

He didn't do anything.

I wiped away my tears as sadness traded for anger. If he thought for a second that he wasn't going to get caught, it was better I found out now.

I blinked my eyes open and groaned, remembering back to when Lucas got jealous of Ethan.

Totally different circumstances.

But it still happened.

The difference here was that Ethan was my transportation and completely uninteresting to me.

Clara and Lucas had been an item. Despite what

he'd said, there had to have been something at some point that attracted him.

The nausea slowly drifted away, and I sat up on the couch, lifting the phone to text.

When were you with Clara?

He wrote back immediately.
Let me call you.

I texted back.
Just tell me.

He texted.

A few weeks ago, she met my brother and me for coffee so I could tell her to quit calling me.

I didn't believe it. Why would you invite someone to coffee to tell them you didn't want to have coffee?

I texted back.

Fine. Call me.

The phone rang instantly, and I picked it up.

"Why didn't you tell me?" I asked.

"This is going to sound insane, but it slipped my mind."

"You're right. It does sound insane. How does something like that slip your mind?"

He let out a deep sigh. "No, you're right. I should have brought it up to you."

"I just don't understand." I felt tears welling up, and I forced them back down.

"She called and left a message the day after you left. I ignored it and went to have lunch with my brother. She called again while we were together, and I told him I couldn't get her to leave me alone."

"And?"

"James thought I should invite her to lunch while he was there since it would be in public, and he could help me tell her to buzz off."

"It obviously worked."

"Damn it, Emily. I'm just such an idiot, and

356

you're not in front of me, so you can't tell that I would do absolutely anything for you. I never meant to hurt you, but I've been so busy wallowing in my own self-pity since you left and I didn't even think about her again. All I think about it is you."

I closed my eyes, hearing the frenzy in his voice, and I knew he was telling the truth.

Of all the men to accuse of stepping out, it shouldn't have been him. Guilt puddled deep in my belly, but I couldn't help it. This long-distance thing was awful.

"Do you believe me?" he asked quietly, and I wanted nothing more than to have him hold me in his arms.

"I believe you, Lucas. I'm sorry for overreacting."

"You don't have anything to apologize for. I'm the nimrod who should have told you about the meeting. It was just so unmemorable that it didn't cross my mind."

"But what she did today has crossed the line. I'll figure something out. I'm going to have my parents call hers. I can't imagine they'd be thrilled to hear this."

"Such a different world you live in," I said offhandedly.

"Emily, I'm truly sorry." He let out a sigh. "Does this set us back?"

"No. I don't think so. I just…" I sighed. "I think I need a little bit of time. Not really because of this, but just because it's all happening so fast, and I'm stuck out here, and you're stuck out there."

"I love you, Emily. I'll fix this."

"I love you too." I hung up and collapsed onto the couch, knowing I needed some time.

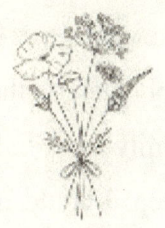

Chapter Twenty-Six

Lucas

I couldn't believe how badly I'd screwed things up. I believed her words that it didn't set us back, but it certainly didn't propel us forward.

All week, I'd respected her wishes and didn't text one message to her.

She needed time, and I was going to give her that.

But I wasn't going to let my flight risk have a reason to soar in the opposite direction of what we could build together.

Hearing the anguish in her voice had undone me, and I wished with every fiber in my being that I'd remembered to tell her that Clara had come to have coffee with us. It sounded reasonable when James devised the plan, and when Clara left, I'd assumed we'd finally put things in the past.

I hung up the phone with the hotel in town where I had arranged for Emily to spend the rest of her time there. She needed sleep. I could hear it in her voice. I could see it when I was there.

The hotel knew that I was sending some packages. I only hoped Emily would take them with the lightness that they were intended.

I'd already reserved a rental car for her that would be delivered to her cabin this afternoon, along with the room key for the hotel.

My phone rang, and I saw it was my father. I answered quickly and stomped toward my bedroom in disgust that I even had to involve my parents, but it also forced me to tell them the entire ordeal I went through, and I was stunned at their level of support and shock.

"Hey, Lucas. I wanted to let you know the next steps."

I took a seat at the end of my bed. "Okay."

"There's really nothing we can do regarding protective orders or anything like that. At the moment, we're just dealing with a nuisance situation."

"That is an understatement," I muttered.

"I know, but our legal team feels strongly that a heavily worded letter, a cease and desist of sorts, will dissuade her from continuing any form of contact. She has a son. Her family won't be thrilled that she's been doing these things." My dad cleared his throat. "But I've forwarded all the screenshots, the timeline of contact, and responses to our team."

"When's the letter going out?"

"We can look at it this evening for approval, and then they'll send it out tomorrow."

I let out a sigh, noticing my knee bobbing.

"Thanks, Dad." I groaned, rubbing my hand over my face in disgust.

"How are things with Emily?"

"She wanted space, and I'm giving it to her." Saying the words suddenly brought the dread I'd been trying to ignore since the call with her last week.

"Oh, I see." My dad went silent for a few seconds. "Is there anything we can do?"

I laughed, shaking my head. "I don't think sending Emily a letter from our legal team would be the best idea."

My dad chuckled, too. "Probably not."

"But I think things are going to be okay. I'm not going to give up on us. I've stayed silent for a year, trying to get her to see the guy I am, and I want to believe that's enough."

"It should be, Son."

"I screwed up royally, though. I really did."

"Emily strikes me as someone who lends grace easily."

"I hope so."

"And I hate to be harsh, but if she can't see how much you love her and that you had no poor intentions with that interaction, you need to find that out now. Not later."

"Yeah. No. I know." I rubbed my eyes and let out a deep breath.

"Alright. Well, I'll send over the letter as soon as I get it later. Oh, and your mom wanted me to tell you that she pulled out one of your grandmother's poetry books and set it on the desk in the study at the orchard. Emily might appreciate seeing it when she returns."

I smiled, thinking about Emily's return and how badly I wanted to see her. "Tell Mom thanks."

"Will do, Lucas."

My dad hung up, and I realized how very different Emily's family and my family were. We didn't express love much by words, more actions, and sometimes those were hard to come by, too, because we were all going in a million different directions.

I thought back to the love oozing out of Mimi's hospital room. They weren't shy in expressing their emotions, which I craved, and I never knew it until Emily.

Walking over to my condo window, I looked out and saw the beautiful city skyline. It had always brought me a sense of satisfaction, and I never imagined wanting to leave it behind.

But I wanted nothing more than to be on Marigold Island, surrounded by friends and family.

I fully understood what made James move to the small island. I also knew I was getting ahead of myself. At this point, I had to convince Emily to even talk to me again.

Obviously, I hadn't given my actions much thought when I kept getting pestered by Clara, and now I was paying the price.

I glanced at my phone on the bed and resisted the temptation to text Emily.

It didn't help that my professional life was also imploding. This morning at the job site, I was slammed with one piece of bad news after another.

The plumber Todd found fell through. The drywall company had to be rescheduled, but now their schedule was booked really far out, which jeopardized our entire timeline. To be safe, we shoved off the Grand Opening, and it all boiled down to costing a lot of money.

I'd always prided myself on never touching my inheritance, but this project worried me.

Then I went to my truck, only to drive about fifty feet and realize I had a flat. I changed it to the spare, but the tire store didn't have the tire in my size, so I had to order it.

I finally got to my condo, only to find out that I had to move out for a week while maintenance did something to the heating system.

And all I could think about was how much I wanted to hold Emily close and wipe my stupid mistake away.

The phone buzzed, and I slowly made my way over because the only person I wanted to hear from wasn't sending communication. I chuckled and shook my head at the irony of it all.

I'd pushed to get out of the platonic wasteland with Emily, and then I screwed things up and wasn't even sure if we'd still be friends.

My heart skipped a beat when I realized that Emily had texted. I scooped my phone up and slid to the message.

I don't know what to say. I'm speechless and forever indebted. I'm so exhausted from not being able to fall asleep at the cabin that I'm at the point of hallucinating. I owe you for this, Lucas.

I sucked on my bottom lip and debated what to text back. Her only priority right now needed to be this residency. None of this drama with Clara. Or worrying about some guy she'd just started dating.

But I didn't want to be just some guy.

What I wanted to do was listen to my heart and fly out to Tennessee to tell her how much I loved her.

As the silence continued on her end, I braced myself for the other alternative. The one where she just couldn't get over my past dating life.

I wanted to believe that wouldn't happen, but the silence said otherwise.

Until now.

My jaw clenched, and I drew in a deep breath as I began a text that I poured my heart and mind into, hoping that I wasn't too late.

***

Emily

If Lucas hadn't arranged for the hotel and car, I didn't know if I'd be able to handle the residency any longer. The nights had stretched into the days, and my poetry felt otherworldly, but only because I couldn't make sense of it at times. But I wouldn't admit any of that to myself.

I was turning my world upside down purely from lack of sleep.

That day that the car showed up and the rental guy handed me the key to the hotel, I knew that Lucas really understood me.

He got me when I didn't even get myself.

Lucas saw that it was exhaustion driving my decisions and reactions. He saw that before I did. I'd become a mess of emotions, and the truth of it was that very little of it had anything to do with Clara. In hindsight, it made sense that he'd try to hash it out with her while his cousin was there.

What threw me over the edge was that I'd done something that I'd been afraid to do for years.

I let myself fall in love.

But not with just anyone.

Someone who meant the world to me.

When I'd finally had my first full night's sleep and woke up the next morning, I knew that I couldn't wait to go home to Lucas, but I needed to focus on this residency. Get my project done with no interruptions.

When the first package arrived from Lucas, I took it to my hotel room and opened the box to see a life-size poster of Lucas and a web address.

I would never forget those feelings that swept through me. Love washed over me that day like I'd never experienced, and he wasn't even in the room. By the time I went to the website, it felt like my heart was going to explode with emotion.

I sat on the plane before it took off, whisking me back home to Marigold Island for good, but I clicked on the video one last time before I landed in Seattle. His booming voice came through my headphones, and my heart immediately swelled.

You're so talented, Emily, and I'm so proud of everything you're accomplishing while you're away. I don't want to become a distraction. We have a lifetime to be there for one another, but I don't want you to look back at this opportunity and wish I wasn't part of it. Just know how much I love you and miss you. You're always free to follow your heart, and I hope it always whispers to come back home to me. I'll be waiting for you.

My heart clenched with the emotion running through his voice, and I couldn't wait to see him again.

To say that absence made my heart grow fonder was an understatement, but I needed the time to prove to myself that I'd made the right choice.

And he knew that.

In the middle of it all, I got this nagging feeling that I had to go somewhere, stay somewhere, and just roam until the feeling went away.

But I didn't realize that was merely fear. I was afraid to let myself imagine a different life.

I wouldn't have known that had I not had the time away. I wish I would have known without the distance, but that wasn't how my heart worked. I needed to hear the whispers of my heart over the screams of my mind.

As our plane hit cruising altitude, I clutched my phone in my hand and drifted to sleep, surprised when we landed in Seattle.

By the time I'd disembarked, my heart raced excitedly, and I knew I had to commit. I had to make my choice.

Chapter Twenty-Seven

Lucas

I knew when she hung up with me that something was off. But I also knew with her in Tennessee and me in Washington, now wasn't the time to pressure her. She already had so much on her plate and there were three weeks left in her program.

So when I got the text a few days later that she needed time, I promised myself that I would give it to her. I vowed not to tarnish the gift she'd been given with the residency. I'd already done damage by foolishly meeting with Clara, thinking I'd put a stop to things.

Unfortunately, I wound up talking to our lawyers, and they suggested sending a strongly worded letter since it was unlikely that anything else could be done.

It seemed to have worked, but my relationship

370

with Emily still hung in the air.

But it was Friday night, and Emily was back on Marigold Island, so I did what any normal almost-ex would do. I went to her favorite hangout spot, found a corner booth, and cracked open my grandmother's poetry book.

And I waited.

Praying the book of poems I had with me would be enough of a sign for Emily.

Every single time the door opened, my gaze would flash to the person walking in, and I started to wonder if maybe Emily wasn't going to show up.

After about an hour, I ordered some garlic fries to go with my beer and kept reading my grandmother's poetry. I thought about the woman who wrote these poems and what she must have seen and experienced in life to create this vivid imagery.

So much like Emily.

As I took another bite of the fries, the door opened and in walked Emily. Her dark hair flowed down her shoulders, and she was wearing a pink halter dress. She carried her book with her as she waved at Rick.

"Your usual, Emily?" he asked.

"Yes, please." She smiled and nodded at the bartender before turning her attention in my direction.

Her gaze latched on mine, and she slowed down.

My heart rate rose fiercely as I swallowed down my worry that she'd suddenly turn around and walk out.

But we weren't that far gone, right?

She straightened her shoulders and kept her gaze on mine, but instead of sitting in my booth, she chose the one next to mine.

I hid a smile and shook my head, knowing the old Emily was back.

Rick brought over her drink and order of garlic fries as I turned my attention back to my book.

After about fifteen minutes of reading more poetry, I heard Emily clear her throat.

"Are you planning on sitting in that booth by yourself all night?" she chided.

"I just might," I shot back. "I'm reading some very good poetry by a woman who goes by Grandma Edwards."

Silence sat between us for a few seconds, and I

wondered if this was my moment to stand up and join her.

Instead, she appeared at my table, and I slid the poetry book to my side.

"What are you doing here?" she asked, her eyes staying on mine.

The instant pull to her nearly consumed me as she sat across from me. Her breaths made the rising and falling of her chest nearly unbearable.

"I actually do like to read."

"So, we have that in common now?"

I nodded. "We always did. I just let you run with your narrative."

Her brows rose as her lips curled slightly.

"And I like staying in lately, more than I like going out," I added.

"I kind of like going out more lately than staying in." She drew a breath, and I forced my gaze to stay on hers.

"I've missed you," I told her, and she smiled.

"I've missed you too." Her eyes stayed focused on me. "But I got my project done. My agent thinks it's got great potential."

"You play the part of the tortured artist well."

She chuckled. "And you?"

"Oh, I figured out my role."

"And what's that?"

"Whatever you need it to be."

She narrowed her eyes on me. "Thank you for getting me a hotel room in town."

I smiled. "Yeah? Did it help?"

Emily laughed. "Tremendously. And I can't thank you enough for the rental car. I couldn't stand the thought of driving around with Ethan one more day. Spit for hair gel doesn't actually smell nice."

I chuckled, shaking my head. "No, I can't imagine it would."

"And most of all, thank you for believing in me." She parted her lips to say more and then closed them.

"You're incredible, Emily."

"I know the last few weeks were hard, but I needed them. I needed the time for me, for my work, and to make sure that when I came back to you, it was because I wanted to, not because it was expected of me."

374

I took a sip of beer.

"But I secretly loved all those messages you sent me so that I knew you understood that we weren't over…"

I nodded, knowing we never would be.

She let out a deep breath. "I never knew that kind of freedom existed, and I never knew that I'd be someone who needed it." Her hand caressed her pendant, and she smiled. "I guess I kind of am like a wildflower at heart."

"I never once doubted it," I said tenderly. "It's why I never pushed you, but I also knew we were meant to be."

She nodded, quietly reflecting, but I knew what she was thinking. Emily was still waiting for that sign.

My hand ran over the smooth cover of my grandmother's poetry book, and I took a deep breath, hoping that this would give her the sign that she so desperately craved.

"Emily, I love you. I'll never stop loving you. You're my best friend, the person I think about night and day. You're my everything. I just can't imagine a world without you in it." I let out a deep breath. "But I need you in my world."

Tears teetered on her lids as she kept her focus on me. "I hope you never for a moment thought I didn't love you, and I don't even think it had to do with Clara."

I smiled, nodding.

"No. I know it didn't." I gripped my grandma's book and slid it onto the table.

Emily's gaze fell to the cover, and she gasped when she saw wildflowers strewn all over. Her fingers traced my grandmother's name as she shook her head, whispering the title.

"Wildflower Fire." She shook her head and stared at me. "This is unbelievable."

I nodded, seeing hope, joy, and exhilaration flood through her gaze.

"I knew there was something more," she whispered. "I always felt it. Some connection with you, but I didn't know why or what."

Emily reached her hand across the table. "We were always meant to be, Lucas. It was written in the stars. It was written in the seeds."

I stood up from the booth and sat next to her,

bringing her close to me as my entire world felt right again.

"Emily, I love you with all I have." My forehead pressed against hers as she traced her fingers along my arms. "And I can't think of anyone else I want as a best friend, as my best friend, as my partner."

"I feel the same way, Lucas. I just love you so much." Her hand ran across the cover of the book, and she smiled. "I can't wait to share this with my sisters and Mom. I'm blown away and freaked out and just... everything feels as right as it did the first time I saw you."

I laughed. "And we both spent a year fighting it, but I'll always be here to support you, Emily. Whatever you want in life, whatever your dreams may be."

"You've more than proven that, Lucas, and I can never thank you enough for giving me the space to be me."

I pressed my lips to hers, and we kissed, finally knowing that we'd be together forever. It was as if the universe had finally spoken, the ghosts of our pasts allowing us to align our futures, and I couldn't imagine this journey with anyone else.

Now, I just couldn't wait to make her my wife.

Chapter Twenty-Eight

Emily

Six months later

I sat in my living room and stared outside as the snowflakes floated to the fluffy white carpet below. Marigold Island never really prepared for snow days, so we all knew to stay inside. Thankfully, I'd stocked up yesterday at the grocery store.

The smell of bacon drifted through the air, and I let out a happy sigh.

"Scrambled eggs or a cheese omelet?" Lucas asked from the kitchen.

I stretched toward the ceiling and pushed the blanket off, feeling more relaxed than I ever had before.

"A cheese omelet," I called back.

So much had changed over the last six months. I no longer felt that anxious energy when I thought about my future. My mind didn't race with opportunities and worries. I didn't spin into needless thoughts about losing my best friend or missing out on my forever.

I had the best of both worlds. Lucas was my everything and more.

There were times when I looked back and realized how lucky I was that he persevered and truly showed me that we could have both. We could be the best of friends and the happiest of couples.

I remembered back to my Grandma Cecilia and thought about the fear she'd had over sharing her poetry and the friendship she lost because of it. The parallels were uncanny, and I could have lost both my best friend and the opportunity to have my happily ever after.

A yowl echoed down the hall, and I froze. What had Oscar gotten into this time?

"Wouldn't you know Brad just happens to be out of town when a storm rolls in?" I hollered to Lucas as I dashed out to follow the shrieking sound. "Dang cat."

The noise led me to the linen closet where Oscar

had perched himself on the top shelf that wasn't really even a shelf. There was only four or five inches between the shelf and the ceiling, and somehow, there was fur feathering between the two, along with a tail and one paw. I didn't even know how he got up there.

I wiped my hands over my mouth and took a deep breath, knowing my odds of having a hand come out of this unscathed were slim to none.

"Hold on, Oscar," I mumbled to the feline and wandered back down the hall to another closet where I'd kept gardening gloves.

Lucas looked gorgeous wearing jeans that hung just right, a fitted tee, and my Valentine's Day apron. He smirked in my direction with a quirked brow. "Everything going okay?"

I held up the gloves and chuckled. "Wish me luck. He's stuck in the linen closet."

Lucas' expression immediately changed. "No. Let me do it."

I scowled at him and glanced at the omelet. "Absolutely not. I won't risk my omelet for Oscar."

"But you'd give up a hand?"

I chuckled and made my way back down the hall, where Oscar's tail had drooped to a discouraging twitch. I grabbed a little step stool and said some encouraging words more for me than him.

"Come on, Oscar," I whispered. "You'll be fine."

A heavy hiss emerged as my hand reached up and around to find his scruff and not his teeth. His hiss turned to a purr, and I panicked.

What was he planning? This cat never purred unless he was ready to attack.

Without thinking, I clenched my eyes shut and pulled him out of the narrow crevice.

My eyes blinked open to see Oscar staring right at me eye to eye.

Lucas came down the hall and smiled. "Omelet is on the table. I'll take it from here."

He knew this was where things got prickly.

I nodded slowly as Lucas gently put his hands over mine, and I let go.

"There you are, Oscar. You're safe now," Lucas said, his voice overly husky. "Now, just don't be a brat at the end here."

I smiled, watching Lucas do the Oscar dance as he went to dump him off on the guest bed as I pulled off my gardening gloves.

Things were calm. Peaceful.

Lucas met me in the hall and swept a kiss across my nose. "There are moments when Oscar is an okay cat."

I chuckled. "Yeah. When he thinks his life is in jeopardy."

I walked to the kitchen to see our breakfast on the table, and my heart warmed. I didn't realize how much I'd craved…this.

Someone to share the little things with as much as the big things.

And I'd had a lot of the big things recently.

In between working at Baubles, my poetry had been picked up by a major publisher, along with a letter of intent for the project based on my Grandma Cecilia. The story was a fictional memoir, kind of experimental with poetry and prose combined, that imagined another way for my Grandma. This story was about what happened had she followed her dreams.

Just the thought made my throat tighten.

"You okay?" Lucas asked, touching my cheek softly.

I sat down in front of my incredible breakfast and nodded. "Yeah. Just thinking about Grandma Cecilia."

"She is so proud of you." Lucas smiled.

"No. Cecilia, not Mimi."

"I know, and I fully believe that your grandma is proud of you because she sees you. She's with you."

I smiled and nodded, feeling his words turn into a warm embrace.

He was right. She was always with me and always would be.

My eyes locked on Lucas, and I shook my head in disbelief. "How did I get so lucky?"

"I'm the lucky one." His eyes stayed steady on mine, and all of those familiar feelings of desire and need rushed through me.

Just like always.

He sat across from me, holding my hand across the table as we enjoyed our omelets and bacon.

It was funny. Before we'd started dating, I always

thought we bickered like an old married couple, poking and prodding at one another, teetering along the boundaries that we each set. But once we started dating, there wasn't an incessant need to push those buttons. We fell into a groove.

I looked down at my plate and realized I'd almost finished my omelet. "A year ago, I never would have guessed that we'd be here…together."

"It's pretty amazing, isn't it?"

"Hey, did you hear from James about our babysitting duties tonight?" I glanced out the kitchen window to see the snowfall heavier. "Do you think they still need us, even with the storm?"

Lucas got a funny look in his eyes and cocked his head slightly.

"What? You heard from him?"

He took a sip of his juice and stood up abruptly. "I can't handle it any longer."

My eyes widened. "Handle what? Babysitting Henry?"

"The moment I met you, I was hooked. I couldn't stop thinking about you. Ask James. I kept hounding him about you while he was with Amelia."

I stared at him, pacing back and forth in the kitchen.

He spun around, smiling. His piercing blue eyes locked on mine.

"Emily, I love you." Lucas shook his head. "I love you more than anything."

"I love you too." My heart started beating a little quicker.

Lucas came over, scooted the chair out, and sat in front of me, pulling my hands to his.

"This isn't how it was supposed to go." His eyes widened, and he looked extra cute. "I had a plan. A big plan."

"Plans are good." I nodded, not knowing where this was headed.

"Emily, you made me dream of the family I never knew I could have. You put me in my place like no one else dared, and you showed me how important it is to listen and embrace your needs, not just my own."

Lucas stood and walked over to the refrigerator. He placed his hand on top, scooted some cereal boxes to the side, and spun back around with one of his grandmother's poetry books in his hand.

He walked back over to me and took a deep breath, kneeling to one knee.

"Emily, I had tonight all planned. I reserved Milo's, and Rick came up with an amazing menu full of garlic fries, chicken tenders, and his famous mini-burgers." He smiled. "And then the storm hit, but I can't wait a single moment longer. I just can't. I need to know if you'll be my wife."

My heart raced as his eyes locked on mine, his words still swirling around me like a dream.

Lucas took my hands in his and placed his grandmother's poetry book in mine, opening to a page with a bookmark.

I gasped when I saw the ring.

"Emily, will you make me the happiest man in the world? Will you marry me? Will you not make me wait a second longer?"

I could feel happy tears threatening to emerge, so I nodded quickly as I squealed yes. I shot out of the chair and pushed myself into his arms, knocking us both to the floor.

He held me tight, and we couldn't stop laughing.

And I knew. This right here was what I needed in a man.

The ability to be my friend and laugh.

Lucas let out a low growl when I slowly rolled off as he untied the ring from the book and slid it on my finger. "I am the luckiest man in the universe, Emily Evans."

Happiness flooded through me as I stared at the man I loved with every part of my being.

"This is my favorite poem, and I thought it described us beautifully," he said softly.

I went to look down to read it, but he cupped my face in his hands first and brought his lips to mine.

His kiss warmed my soul, and I knew how lucky I was to have found a man who understood me and who I understood.

When his lips parted from mine, I looked down to see the words on the page, and my breath hitched with its beauty. This was a book I didn't know about.

You were never meant to be caught, my little wildflower,

Petals as vibrant as the sun,

But tender to the touch of some,

You spread beauty for everyone to see,

But I beg you to be with me

In a field where you can roam

And feel so free

Lucas' gaze caught mine with tears in my eyes. He kissed me again, and I knew he was my home.

Dear Readers,

Thank you so much for reading the second book in the Curiosity Bay Series! I hope you absolutely loved the story of Emily and Lucas! It's so much fun to go back to Marigold Island and visit the Evans sisters and getting to write a friendship-to-more book was a blast. I'm so grateful that you've been so supportive of this new series and have shared the love of Curiosity Bay with friends and family. And as always, thank you for the positive ratings and reviews. Always appreciated! *Tempting the Heart* is up next and follows Mae and her first love…

Warmest wishes,
Karice

KARICE BOLTON BOOKS

CURIOSITY BAY SERIES
HEART OF CURIOSITIES
WILDS OF THE HEART
TEMPTING THE HEART

THE SUNSHINE BREAKFAST CLUB SERIES
DASH OF LOVE
PINCH OF LOVE
SPRINKLE OF LOVE
CHRISTMAS OF LOVE
SMIDGE OF LOVE

CLOUDBERRY INN SERIES
IMAGINING YOU
REMEMBERING YOU
LEAVING YOU
LOVING YOU

MR. MISTAKE SERIES
MR. MISTAKE
MR. ACCIDENT
MR. WRONG
MR. RIGHT

ISLAND COUNTY SERIES
FINDING LOVE IN FORGOTTEN COVE
LOVE REDONE IN HIDDEN HARBOR
TANGLED LOVE ON PELICAN POINT
FOREVER LOVE ON FIREWEED ISLAND
TEMPTING LOVE ON HOLLY LANE

CHANCE AT LOVE ON MYSTIC BAY
IRRESISTIBLE LOVE AT SILVER FALLS
LUCKY IN LOVE ON HOUND ISLAND
MISTLETOE MISCHIEF
ACCIDENTAL LOVE ON MEADOW COVE LANE
DISCOVERING LOVE ON CRANBERRY LANE
CHRISTMAS ON FIREWEED
IMAGINING LOVE ON FIREWEED
CHRISTMAS CRUSH ON FIREWEED ISLAND
WAITING LOVE AT HAWTHORNE AVENUE
FOREVER CHRISTMAS ON SUGARPLUM LANE

BEYOND LOVE SERIES
BEYOND CONTROL
BEYOND DOUBT
BEYOND REASON
BEYOND INTENT
BEYOND CHANCE
BEYOND PROMISE
BEYOND the MISTLETOE

SILVER RIDGE SERIES
A HAPPY TRUTH ABOUT LOVE
A LITTLE SECRET ABOUT LOVE
A FUNNY THING ABOUT LOVE
A SURPRISING FACT ABOUT LOVE
A SIMPLE WISH ABOUT LOVE
CHRISTMAS AT SILVER RIDGE

LUKE FLETCHER SERIES
HIDDEN SINS
BURIED SINS
REDEMPTION

MIA

V MAFIA SERIES
BLAKE
DEVIN
JAXSON

THE WITCH AVENUE SERIES
LONELY SOULS
ALTERED SOULS
RELEASED SOULS
SHATTERED SOULS

THE WATCHERS TRILOGY
AWAKENING
LEGIONS
CATACLYSM
TAKEN NOVELLA (A Watchers Prequel)

AFTERWORLD SERIES
RecruitZ
AlibiZ
UprisingZ

BLOOD TORN DUET
BLOOD TORN
BLOOD CURSED